REMARKABLE

═◐ Ernest Pickle's ◑═
REMARKABLE

MAX DANN

illustrated by David Pearson

STARLIGHT

A Starlight Book

This edition published in Australia and New Zealand in 1995
by Hodder Headline Australia Pty Limited,
(A member of the Hodder Headline Group)
10-16 South Street, Rydalmere NSW 2116

First published in 1984 by Oxford University Press
Reprinted in 1985, 1986, 1988, 1989, 1990

National Library of Australia Cataloguing-in-Publication data

Ernest Pickle's remarkable robot.

ISBN 0 7336 0069 7.
1. Children's stories, Australian. I. Pearson, David.
II. Title.

A823.3

Printed by Griffin Paperbacks
Cover illustration by David Pearson

1

It was time. Ernest Pickle opened the shed door a fraction and peeped out up at the house. No sign of anyone coming. His mum and Number Two were in the front room playing Scrabble. That always kept them busy for a while.

Ernest walked back across to his creation and pulled the blanket off. Even with just the one dim light globe, it glowed. It was bright gold, a shiny gold metal. He'd finally finished it. A walking, talking, life-size robot. Ernest went about activating the link-up terminals and making a few last-minute checks.

The robot stood more than a full head taller

than Ernest. It had arms, legs, feet and hands like a man, but it didn't look so much like a man that it would pass for one. It had elbow joints and finger joints and knee-caps made of plastic. Its face was half-metal, half-plastic, with inbuilt 99.03 per cent acute accuracy hearing, sight and smell sensors.

Ernest had decided to call him Glen, after Gyroscopically-Linked Equivalence Network.

Glen had already memorised and understood all the knowledge found in an average-sized library. He could speak and read in twenty-one foreign languages, and recite the entire Oxford Dictionary word for word. Ernest had been programming him constantly for the last few days.

While he had been completing the final station links, he had plugged Glen up to cassette programs. He had played him tapes on World Statistics, History, Physics, Advanced Science, Modern Psychology, Paranormal Phenomena, Hang-Gliding, Geography, One Hundred and One Fancy-Dance Steps, Einstein's Theory of Relativity,

Glen takes his first steps: part one

Newton's Law of Gravity, Astronomy, Astrology, How to Build an Aeroplane in 8,123 Easy Steps, The Industrial Revolution, Gardening, Advanced Technology, Known Wildlife, Engineering, Anthropology, Burt Reynolds' Biography, Famous Sporting Events, and Geology. Glen had even read four boxes of *Home and Garden* magazines that Ernest's mum had stored in the shed.

That wasn't all, of course. The list went on and on. There was much more to come. Ernest had only just begun to load Glen's data banks.

Ernest stepped back a little, and spoke to Glen for the first time.

'Hello Glen,' Ernest said. 'Are you there?'

There was no reply for thirty seconds, then: 'Who's that?' Glen asked quietly.

2

Just a multi-processor

Ernest had been building Glen for almost six months. He had worked on him solidly every night after school, on weekends, even first thing in the mornings. Ernest never went out, never watched television, never played games, never read books (unless they were on robotics); he never did anything except work out in the shed. And when he wasn't working, he would padlock his half of the shed. He kept his work to himself.

Number Two shared the other half of the shed. Number Two was Ernest's second dad. His first father, Number One, had left home in a huff eight years before when Ernest was

Just a multi-processor

three years old, and hadn't been heard of since. According to Ernest he had been 'quite tall, and smelt like cigars all the time'.

Number Two was entirely different. He was short and bald, and brushed his teeth probably twenty-five times a day. Whenever Number Two was worried or anxious about something he would brush his teeth. Number Two smelt like peppermint toothpaste.

He worked as a technical adviser and researcher at a company called C.I.T.I. Computer Software Development Corporation. He brought bits and pieces of computer components home for Ernest to play with: diodes, micro-chips, readout screens, that sort of thing.

Ernest had a way with computers. He didn't seem to even have to try to understand how they worked. It was just something he knew. He subscribed to several computer magazines such as *Micro-System* and *Computer News*. Not only could he understand the magazines, he knew most of the information in them already.

Ernest had to have a way with something. He wasn't very good at anything else. He couldn't play football, or cricket, or volleyball. He was a terrible Scrabble player, couldn't draw, didn't understand crosswords or jigsaw puzzles, didn't get along very well with animals, and was terrible at parties. However, his worst problem was other people. In eleven years he hadn't been able to make one friend. He'd made two or three enemies without even trying, but making friends was impossible.

People seemed to ignore him. The reason for this was a complete mystery to Ernest. It wasn't as if he was unfriendly to people. He was always trying to start up conversations. He offered them his advice on this and that, spoke at length on politics, read interesting passages out of his computer magazines, discussed news items. But nobody seemed particularly interested.

Just the other day, for example, when he had started to describe to Robert how his watch worked (a fairly interesting topic),

Robert had simply turned around and said:

'How come you're always so boring, Ernest?'

Robert was the nearest thing Ernest had to a friend. At least Robert answered him (sometimes). There was Elizabeth, too, of course. Ernest fancied himself and Elizabeth as almost being friends. At least they would have been if they'd talked to each other. They would say hello to each other and smile, but Ernest could never think of anything to say to her after that.

Ernest admired Elizabeth from afar, usually from the other side of the quadrangle, or across the classroom. She was friendly, and funny, and brave. She did a lot of dangerous sports, such as basketball, scuba diving and cycling. It was a pity they didn't have anything in common to talk about, Ernest thought.

So he never bothered her with himself. Besides, Elizabeth had friends all over school. He didn't imagine she would care one way or another about having another friend. Especially not him.

While Number Two went on fiddling about in his side of the shed, trying to perfect his miniature electric toothbrush with the FM radio built in to the handle, Ernest threw himself into his inventions. He had invented quite a few things before, but nothing like Glen.

He had started off with just a multi-processor and a series of feeder pick-ups in a box. He'd been going to bolt this arrangement to a bench and wheel it around. However, as he went on experimenting, he'd begun to realise Glen's true potential. Legs, arms and a head were added. Soon Glen had capabilities far exceeding those of a machine that simply processed and calculated information; he had abilities far exceeding those of a robot that could move about independently. Glen was a masterpiece.

Glen could think, have feelings and emotions, and he performed feats that no other machine, or human, had been able to do before. Ernest had built more than just a friend: he had big plans for Glen. Glen was going to help him make friends with all those people who ignored and disliked him. Glen was the best thing he had ever made. He was going to change Ernest's life.

Then there was his birthday party to think about, too.

3

He could speak! Glen spoke perfectly! Ernest was so excited he didn't know what to say next. He thought for a moment and then said:

'I'm your maker.'

'Dad!' Glen exclaimed.

'No, no, I'm not your dad. I only made you.'

'God?'

'No, I'm Ernest. Just plain Ernest.'

Ernest could see there was still a lot he had to fill Glen in on. While he knew everything there was to know about some things, he knew practically nothing at all about others.

'How do you feel?' Ernest asked him in big

slow words.

'To tell you the truth, I feel a touch giddy. Do you mind if I lie down?'

Ernest cleared the bench for him.

'I think it is my inner-drive gears. They are set a little fast.'

Ernest helped him up on to the bench. Glen stretched out on his back and lay staring up at the ceiling.

'Does that feel any better?'

'Slightly.'

'I'll re-time the gears later,' Ernest said.

'Thank you Dad, I would appreciate it.'

'I'm not your dad! Just plain Ernest.'

'Sorry, Pop.'

Ernest went and got the photo albums out of the house. He had to straighten Glen out on a few things.

'You see,' he said when he got back, 'we're not actually related at all. I know you've listened to tapes about families and relatives, but we're not brothers or cousins, or father and son, or anything like that. I built you out of bits and pieces. We're entirely different from each other.'

'I was wondering why you weren't made out of metal,' Glen said.

'That's because you are a machine. I made you, so that I could have a friend, and—'

'Friend. Friend,' Glen repeated, as if he liked the sound of that particular word over the others.

'I don't have any friends.' Ernest paused. 'Nobody likes me.'

'But now you have me.'

Ernest didn't seem to hear him.

'I'm having a party soon. My mum and Number Two are forcing me to. I've told them it's quite useless. I've told them I don't have any friends, but they don't believe me.'

'I'll come.'

Ernest had stopped listening to Glen. He was talking to himself now.

'They asked me to write a list of people I'd like to invite, who I think might come. So I did, but there's not enough people on it for a party.'

Ernest showed Glen his list. It said:

Glen takes his first steps: part two

PARTY INVITATIONS

Elizabeth

~Robert~

'I've changed my mind about Robert. It's just Elizabeth now.'

'Elizabeth? Is that some sort of club?' Glen asked.

'It's just the one person. If I had a photo I'd show you.' Ernest paused and thought for a moment. His eyes took on a distant look. 'She's got hair,' he continued, 'that's so dark and curly and long it's like streamers. And her chin is sort of pointy, English, I think. My chin is square, French, I think. They say opposites attract. And you can tell she's got a healthy attitude to life because she smiles nearly all the time. She bought me an ice cream once, when I didn't even know her at all. That was quite generous, I think.'

Ernest went on day-dreaming for a moment longer, then suddenly snapped out of it. He opened up the first of the photo albums and began showing Glen photos of his mum,

Number Two, Ernest himself, the house, the car, even their annual holidays. He explained things about them as they went. Glen asked a lot of questions, mostly about the house. He seemed to have developed an interest in architecture. It probably had something to do with all the *Home and Garden* magazines. 'At least he'll have something to talk about with my mother,' Ernest thought. She was always talking about remodelling the house.

'How many bedrooms does the house have?' Glen asked.

'Three,' Ernest answered, once they were finished with the photos. 'Now, I have these books here I want you to read.' Ernest lifted a box full of books he'd borrowed from the library up on to the bench beside Glen.

'Who sleeps in the third bedroom?' Glen asked.

'It's a spare room. Now, I want you to read these—'

'How would you describe the house, classic Edwardian style or more—'

'Edwardian!' Ernest snapped. He decided

the *Home and Garden* magazines had been a mistake. He emptied the books out of the box, and stacked them up in front of Glen.

'It's important that you read these,' Ernest said to him.

They had titles such as *The Human Thought Patterns, Subconscious Thought Transferral, Frequencies—The Invisible Messages, How To Meet and Influence People, The Human Brain, Hypnotism and Its Lasting Effects,* and *Extra-Sensory Perception.*

'Heavy reading,' Glen said, looking at the spines. 'You haven't got anything on house design, have you?'

'I haven't made a robot, I've built an architect!' Ernest sighed.

Number Two called out then. He had a way of standing at the back door and calling out TIME FOR BED so that the whole neighbourhood knew it was time for Ernest to go to bed.

'I have to go up and go to sleep now, before anybody gets suspicious. You'll have to stay here. I don't think you're ready to be introduced to the outside world yet.'

'Which one is your bedroom?'

'Third window along on the apple-tree side. I'll call back first thing in the morning. You should have finished reading all the books by then. Do you need the light on?'

'No, thank you.'

Ernest had forgotten for a moment that Glen had his own light.

'Goodnight, then.'

'Goodnight.'

Ernest went up to the house and left Glen reading.

It was sometime in the middle of the night when Ernest happened to roll over. He touched something cold. There was something icy and steely smooth in his bed with him. He leapt up and switched on his bedside light.

It was Glen! Lying down next to him! Right in between the sheets and everything! (Ernest didn't like sharing his bed.)

'What are you doing in my bed?'

'I thought you might want some company.'

Glen takes his first steps: part two

'Not when I'm sleeping! What would I want company for when I'm asleep?'

'I was cold out in the shed.'

'Cold? How can you get cold? You're all metal and plastic!'

'My sensors informed me that the temperature had dropped to a low 4.74 degrees Celsius. According to my calculations, that is quite cold.'

'But robots don't sleep.'

'I was resting my inner gears. You forgot to re-adjust them.'

'Sorry. Did you finish the books?'

'I felt too giddy.'

'I'll fix you in the morning. It's important that you read those books,' Ernest reminded him. 'Well, I suppose you may as well stay here tonight, now that you're here. But don't go getting used to it. Tomorrow night you sleep somewhere else.'

'Thank you.'

Ernest went and put on a second pair of pyjamas and got back into bed. He didn't want to lean up against Glen and get a chill.

4
Breakfast

'**A***AAAAAAAAH!*'

Ernest woke up to a screech so loud and piercing it ran up and down the length of his spine like a stampede. His ears felt like they were being twisted off. He sat straight up. His mum's footsteps ran past his door, down the hall, and into the next bedroom, where Number Two was still sleeping.

'What?' Number Two said sleepily.

There was no use trying to keep it a secret now. Glen had woken up early.

By the time Ernest got out of bed and into his dressing-gown, his mum and Number Two were already in the kitchen. Glen was introducing himself to them and they were standing staring at him, fixed where they were. Screwed down to the spot.

'I've been looking around the house,' Glen was saying. 'Quite a plain design, but the practicality of it certainly appeals to me. The dining room connecting with the kitchen on one side and the living room on the other is very impressive. Yes, I like that idea. I think the double doors really add to the effect of spaciousness. And having the living room open into the hall, with the bedrooms opposite, is quite unusual.'

'I designed that,' Ernest's mum squeaked.

'You did? That is just the way I would have designed it! Great minds think alike. The bedrooms are well set out too. Of course our room is a little small—'

'Our room?' Number Two repeated stupidly.

'Ernest's and mine. The doorway just off the bathroom.' Ernest arrived at that moment. 'Oh, there's my maker! Good morning, Just Plain Ernest.'

'It's not Just Plain Ernest!'

'Oh, sorry, Dad.'

'I'm not your dad, either!'

'Ernest,' Number Two leaned over and whispered in his ear, 'who's the crackpot?'

'My name is Glen. I'm sorry I didn't introduce myself. How rude, I thought I had.'

'I made him,' Ernest said. 'I was going to break it to you slowly.' He paused and glared across at Glen. 'He got up before I could stop him.'

'But what, exactly, is it?' Number Two whispered.

'Some sort of—' his mum started.

'He's a robot,' Ernest announced. He felt a swelling sensation in his chest. It could have been pride, but he wasn't sure. He wasn't used to such a feeling. 'He's my masterpiece,' he added.

'Why, he moves and talks independently!' Number Two went on whispering.

'In twenty-one different languages,' Glen butted in.

'He also hears conversations up to four

kilometres away. There's no point trying to whisper,' Ernest said.

'He really *is* a robot!' his mum said.

'Ernest, you're a genius!' Number Two added.

'Yes, I'm quite revolutionary,' Glen started again. 'I believe there have been various prototype models constructed before me, but with little success. I understand the most common difficulty was in linking independent motivational response to a sufficiently sophisticated processing centre. Ernest, however, overcame this through a combination of innovative modification and re-adaption of pre-existing available systems. Of course Ernest ran into some difficulties as well, mainly with my inner-drive gears. He adjusted them too fast.'

'This is fantastic!' Number Two muttered.

'Yes, I was quite surprised when I realised this myself,' Glen continued. 'Because of the required precision in such a delicate arrangement of gears, it would seem unlikely that I could function at all in this present state of neglect. However, apart from some sluggishness in my scanner gates and my dizzy spells, I appear to be operating almost normally.'

'Does he ever stop talking?' Ernest's mum asked.

'Oh no, I can go on talking like this indefinitely,' Glen said. 'I find the energy output of conversation extremely low. It's draining effect on my reserve banks is less than negligible.'

'He's just getting used to the sound of his own voice,' Ernest said.

'How about some breakfast?' Glen offered. 'I found an interesting recipe in one of the cook books on top of the refrigerator.'

'The Indian books?' Ernest's mum said.

'Yes, Fruity Curried Eggs,' Glen announced.

'Fruity Curried Eggs?' Number Two said.

'Sound delicious, don't they? I made up some curry powder while you were asleep, and I've managed to find most of the other ingredients. I couldn't locate any mango chutney, but I thought we could quite easily substitute banana chutney. I know it's not quite the same, but since the recipe calls for so little of it—'

Glen went on chatting all through breakfast.

'He's just going through a talkative stage,' Ernest explained to his mum and Number Two.

Glen went on and on. He spoke about the marketing strategies for battery eggs, the expected life-span of the average chicken, Marxism, Freud's theory of dreams, and the printing of modern newspapers. He was still talking as Ernest left for school, when he was back on his favourite subject, architecture. As Ernest walked out the door, Glen was discussing Gothic Relief with Ernest's mum.

5
— School life —

Ernest was so excited thinking about Glen when he left home that he forgot to cross the road before he got to Rowena's place. Rowena lived behind the butcher's shop on the corner, and had a habit of hiding, waiting for him in her doorway.

She jumped out in front of Ernest as he was passing, with her dog Butch who was snarling and pulling on his lead trying to get at him.

'Hah! Did I scare you?'

The sight of Rowena was enough to send shivers the size of locomotives up the back of Ernest's neck. She had tight, short white hair, narrow slits for eyes, and jagged little teeth. Rowena had the sense of humour of a black widow spider, and the personality of an eclipse. She wanted to be a terrorist when she grew up. She also happened to be one of Ernest's three enemies. Rowena was enemy number one.

'Thought you were going to slip by me, I suppose?'

Ernest stopped where he was. Rowena stalked in a circle around him.

'No,' Ernest answered meekly.

'Yes you did.'

He wasn't going to argue with her. She'd stopped in front of him now, and was holding Butch's lead out, just far enough away so Ernest could feel the wind of Butch's jaws snapping open and close.

'I've got a present for you,' Rowena teased in her sing-song voice. Then in a harsher voice she yelled, 'Sit!'

Butch, a bull-terrier, sat. Rowena handed Ernest the lead.

'Here, hold this a minute and I'll get it.'

Ernest looked down at Butch. He was panting and dribbling, and his tongue was rolling back and forth across his teeth. Butch was looking at Ernest's leg. It had occurred to Ernest that Rowena looked a lot like Butch. He'd never mentioned it, though.

'Hold on with both hands,' Rowena ordered. 'He's strong.'

Ernest made the mistake of putting his bag down to do it. This was what Rowena had been waiting for. She pulled a paper bag out from somewhere behind her, and emptied whatever was in it into his school bag. Ernest dropped the lead and looked down.

Tongues! She'd emptied a bag of lambs' tongues all over his books! They were all different slippery shapes and sizes.

'I got my dad to save them up for you,' she cackled.

Then while Ernest was still bending over, she slid a sheep's brain down the back of his shirt, slapped him between the shoulder blades, and cracked a rotten egg over his head.

'Ha! Ha! Ha! Ha! Sick him, Butch!'

Ernest barely had enough time to pick up his bag of tongues and escape. Once he was away he was impossible to catch. Ernest was a fast runner—he was compared with Rowena and Butch, anyway. They both had little short legs and thick bodies. He left them way behind.

Ernest didn't stop until he reached the school gate. He walked the rest of the way in and across the quadrangle, passing Robert half way across.

'Hiya', Robert.'

Robert just nodded and kept on walking. Ernest kept on walking too. He went over to the toilet block to wash his hair out. On his way he stopped and sat next to Pauline Jenkins and Jim Murphy for a minute. They were playing around with Pauline's new calculator.

'New calculator?' Ernest asked.

They just went on talking between themselves.

'Guess what?' he tried a moment later. When they didn't bother trying to guess, he told them anyway. 'I've built myself a robot.'

'Yeah,' Jim Murphy said flatly. He sounded half asleep. 'What's it do?'

'Practically everything: processes, calculates, thinks, walks, talks. Like a person.'

'Yeah,' Jim Murphy said again.

They weren't interested. 'I might as well not be talking at all,' Ernest thought to himself.

He stood up and left them and went on to the toilets. He should have walked on down to the taps by the shelter sheds instead, because Rex Surley and his friend Colin Carter were in the toilets. They were trying to pull off the tap handles to make belt buckles. Rex and Colin were his other two enemies. Ernest turned around to walk out again quickly but they spotted him before he had a chance to get away.

'Hold it, Pickle! Where do you think you're going?' Rex growled.

Ernest stopped where he was. It wasn't a good idea to try and make a break for it. They would only be twice as nasty on him if they had to go to the trouble of catching him as well.

'I was just going to use one of the taps,' Ernest muttered.

'Well, don't let us stop you,' Rex purred.

'I can see you're busy with them right now. I'll come back later.'

'Come on in, Pickle!'

They had both stopped what they were doing, and were leaning with their backs against the basins looking at him. Ernest took two steps forward.

'You're not scared, are you?' Rex said.

Rex was big for his age. He was tall, and had a big, awkward, bony sort of body.

('He looks like he's still trying to figure out how it all works,' Number Two had said on the parent-teacher night he'd seen him.)

Rex had an annoying habit of always pretending he was in a boxing ring with the person unlucky enough to be talking to him. He'd dance around, duck, jab you in the chin, feint, swipe you across the ear, do a bit of a jig. Even if Ernest had wanted to box back it would have been hopeless. Rex had arms which were at least thirty centimetres longer than those of normal people. He was like a rotary hoist.

'You're not spying on us, are you, Pickle?' Rex said, then ducked as if Ernest were throwing a punch at him.

'What's that stuff all over you?' Colin Carter asked. 'It stinks.'

Colin was small and mean, like a rat. He had a little mouth and little eyes, and big ideas about himself. His favourite pastime was picking fights and then calling on Rex to help him.

'It's egg,' Ernest muttered.

'It suits you,' Rex said.

'What did you do, miss your mouth?' Colin nearly choked to death laughing at his own joke.

'Rowena did it.'

'We don't want to know your personal problems, Pickle,' Rex snarled as he picked up Ernest's bag and threw it up on to the toilet roof. Ernest heard it land with a thud, out of sight. He thought of the tongues; they were going to be all through his books now.

'Sorry, was that your bag?' Rex asked mockingly.

Ernest looked up thoughtfully at the roof. 'It doesn't matter,' he said.

'Well, what are you going to do about it?'

'It's just a bag,' Ernest shrugged.

'You're so weak, Pickle, it's disgusting. Sometimes, I don't know why, I almost feel ashamed picking on you. It's not just that you're a miserable jerk, but you're such a wimp as well.' He pushed Ernest against a door, and held him pinned there. 'But I just can't help myself when it comes to you.'

Before they left they tied Ernest up to one of the latrine doors with his jumper and some rope they'd found and left him suspended there, swinging backwards and forwards.

'Nobody will miss him.'

'Nobody even knows he's here in the first place,' Rex said. They both laughed and went into class.

Ernest might have gone on hanging there

until morning recess if Glen hadn't turned up. He walked into the toilets dressed in one of Number Two's overcoats and carrying a plain brown paper bag in his hand.

'You forgot your lunch,' Glen said.

'How did you find me?' Ernest asked.

'Sensory identification. I followed the sound of your heart beat.' Glen took a closer look at the way Ernest was tied to the door. 'Is this what you do all day at school? How do you eat your lunch?'

'This is just a prank. Can you get me down, please Glen?'

Glen extended one hand and touched the rope with the tips of his fingers. In a moment they heated up and smoked their way through the twine like a soldering iron. He worked his way around until Ernest could free himself.

'Thanks, Glen.'

'My pleasure, Ernest.'

'Now there's just my bag on the roof. Do you think you could get it down for me?'

'Which one it is?'

'It'll be the only one up there. Rex threw it

up. He gets a kick out of that sort of thing.'

'Oh, allow me.'

Glen pointed his other arm upwards. He extended its length, until it was level with the roof guttering. Then he activated the magnetic drive in his palm, and the bag slid across and into his fingers. It was drawn over by its metal fittings.

Ernest washed, emptied the tongues out of his bag, and walked with Glen across the yard—

'Umm, stucco effect,' Glen commented on the school building.

—and into the classroom.

'Good morning, Mr Carruthers,' Ernest said. Mr Carruthers was the class teacher. 'Sorry I'm late. I got tied up in the toilets.'

Mr Carruthers didn't seem to care. He had the 'flu. He always had something wrong with him. He caught things from the students. If there was something going around, he would catch it. And there was always something going around. He was slumped over his desk like a tired vulture.

'Who's the new boy?' he asked sleepily. He didn't bother taking anything more than a passing glance at Glen.

'Glen. He's with me. I made him at home.'

'Has he registered at the office yet?' He spoke without lifting his chin from his hands.

'He's not a human, he's a robot. I built him myself.'

'Another one of your contraptions. I asked you not to bring any more to school with you, Ernest.'

Ernest had brought things he'd made to school before, such as the battery-operated deck-chair, the electronically-controlled dustbin (its lid lifted off with the push of a button), the self-watering pot plant, the remote-control revolving hat and coat stand, and the self-answering phone-table. Ernest often brought his inventions to school to show everyone, not that anyone was ever interested.

'I couldn't help it, Sir,' Ernest said. 'He came here all by himself.'

'All right,' Mr Carruthers said to Glen, 'find somewhere to sit down and get to your

School life

desk. Up by Elizabeth will do.'

Ernest watched as Glen went and took the seat next to Elizabeth. Being seated beside Elizabeth had been Ernest's ambition all year. Elizabeth sat up the back. Ernest had tried every excuse to be placed back there with her: short-sightedness, allergic reactions to chalk dust ... he'd even complained about draughts coming in under the door. He was practically positive that he would be able to think of something to say if he sat next to her for long enough. Now Glen was sitting next to her and he hadn't been in the class for five minutes.

'I should have been born a machine,' he mumbled to himself unhappily as he took his seat next to Judith Walker. She was a skinny girl with a pointed face and a receding chin who only talked to him when she needed to borrow one of his pens.

Elizabeth was the only one in the class who took any notice of Glen. Rex snuck a punch in as Glen walked past him, but he hurt his hand on the metal plate and lost interest. One or two others glanced around at him, but as far as they were concerned he was just another stupid machine of Ernest's.

But Elizabeth couldn't take her eyes off Glen. This one was different. He could walk around by himself, for one thing. And he could talk!

'I'm very pleased to meet you. My name is Glen.'

Glen held out his hand. Elizabeth looked at it for a while before she did anything with it. Finally she shook it.

'I'm gyroscopically driven through a solar bank,' Glen started. He had been played a tape on Correct Procedure For Introductions, and this was the first girl he had ever met. 'My data processing capabilities are in excess of 5000 words per minute. I am impervious to sudden and all extreme temperature changes. I do not rust, age, peel, or fray. And my hobby is architecture.'

'Are you really a robot?'

'Apparently. I thought I may have been a relative of Ernest's, but according to data gathered since, I'm not.'

Elizabeth paused and thought. She had a habit of thinking things out before she said anything. 'Do I talk back to you?'

'Please do,' Glen said.

'What do I talk to you about?'

'Anything, really. My reserve storage facilities cover quite a large range of topics. And I'm a sensible listener as well.'

'Just normal, people sort of things then?'

'Anything.'

Elizabeth looked over at Ernest. He was doodling in his English book. He looked even more depressed than usual. Apart from everything else, his breakfast was repeating on him.

'The trouble is,' she began, 'nobody understands Ernest. You can tell he's smart just from looking at him, don't you think so?'

'Oh undoubtedly yes.'

'Did he really make you? He didn't assemble you out of a kit or anything?'

'Component by component.'

'I just don't understand why somebody so clever has to be so unhappy too.'

'Bad diet I suspect,' Glen said, 'but I plan to correct that.'

'He certainly does look pale.'

'Oh undoubtedly so.'

Elizabeth paused again to think, then said, 'How am I doing? Can you understand what I'm talking about?'

'Oh yes, as a matter of fact you speak more clearly than Ernest. He mumbles terribly—'

'*Elizabeth!*' Mr Carruthers shouted. 'Will you stop talking to Ernest's contraption and get on with your work please!'

6

The party

The very minute Ernest arrived back home from school in the afternoon, his mum brought up the subject of the birthday party again. It had taken him practically all day to forget about it. He was hoping that if he didn't say anything about it, the whole rotten idea would be forgotten.

'Your father will get the invitations printed tomorrow,' his mum said.

'I won't be needing many.'

'Well, just write down the names of the people you'd like to invite so that we'll know how many to have done.'

'I'd really rather not have a party,' Ernest

grumbled. 'Nobody will come anyway. There's no point in inviting anybody. Besides, I don't like parties.'

'Oh, don't be so pessimistic, Ernest. You'll have a wonderful time. You can invite all your friends from school and up the street.'

'I don't have any friends.'

'Of course you do, Ernest. Everybody has friends.'

'Not me.'

'Don't exaggerate. For instance, you could ask Robert and Pauline. And what about Rex and his friend Colin? They seemed like nice boys the night I met them. Then there is Rowena down on the corner—'

'Excuse me, Mum,' Ernest interrupted, 'I have to go down and do some work on Glen in the shed. He's waiting for me.'

Ernest picked up his cup of chocolate milk and slipped down to the shed.

Down at the shed Ernest re-adjusted Glen's gears, then flopped down on to an old crate and stared away into the distance.

'Oh, that does feel better,' Glen said as he

strolled around the shed a couple of times. 'One hundred per cent. I was beginning to think I was going to feel giddy the rest of my life. Oh yes, it's a pleasure to stand up now.'

'I need you to read those books I gave you as soon as possible,' Ernest said, glumly preoccupied.

'Do I have to?'

'My future depends on it. I have to program you in time for the party.'

'Program me to do what, Ernest?'

'My life is going to change. Nobody is going to push me around or ignore me any more. I'm going to have friends, lots of friends, maybe more friends than anybody has ever had before.'

A small, single tear streaked from a corner of one of his eyes, and made a tiny snail's track down his face. 'I'll have so many people come to this party they won't all be able to fit in the house. They'll have to stand in a queue outside. And they'll all like me.'

Glen put a heavy hand on Ernest's shoulder.

'I like you,' he said.

Ernest barely heard him. After all, no matter how clever he was, or what capabilities Glen had, he was still just a machine.

Ernest made Glen stay at home while he went to school the following day. He wanted Glen to read all the books.

'It's important that you memorise them, word for word,' Ernest said. 'Put them on your easy-access file, set yourself on probe analysis and expanded thought channels.'

Ernest went to school and decided to let one or two people know about his party. 'It won't do any harm,' he thought.

'My mum and Number Two are throwing me a party,' he told Robert.

'That's nice.' Robert seemed more interested in a stone he had caught in the tread of his shoe.

'Probably be food and games and that sort of thing,' Ernest went on. He cleared his throat three times before saying, 'Will you come?'

'Naw, I'll probably be too busy. When is

The party

it?'

'Next week.'

'Yeah, I'm busy next week.'

'Oh well, never mind. It doesn't matter. Maybe next year.'

'Yeah, maybe. Ask me then.'

Ernest didn't feel like mentioning the party to anybody else after that, not even to Elizabeth, especially not to Elizabeth. He was depressed enough. If Elizabeth had said she was too busy as well he wouldn't have been able to go on living.

7

African Elephant

Glen was helping Number Two with his toothbrush when Ernest got home.

'Glen has come up with a new way of installing the aerial in the far end of the handle,' Number Two was saying from over the sink. He was trying it out. 'It doesn't poke you in the nose any more,' he said through a mouthful of peppermint froth.

'That's nice.'

'If only I could work out the volume. I think the speaker needs to be shifted. I need to move it right away from the bristles—I can't hear a thing. Say, Ernest, have you given any more thought about how many you'd like to invite?'

'Still thinking.'

'There's no need to be nervous. Just invite as many as you want. I'll get about two hundred invitations printed. I know we won't use them all, but what we don't use now we can use next year. I remember my first party. I was convinced nobody was going to come. I thought I was going to have a heart attack—'

Ernest didn't hear the rest. He gestured to Glen to follow him over to his half of the shed. Ernest locked the door after them.

'Did you read the books?'

'What books?'

'The books! The books!'

'Oh, *those* books. Yes, Ernest, but I've been wondering why you—'

'Did you switch yourself on to your expanded thought channels?'

'Yes, Ernest. But why all those books about the same thing ...?'

Ernest started clearing the bench. 'Okay, let's get started then. I need to get into your main station crossovers and rear relay terminals. You'd better lie down.'

Ernest worked through most of the evening. He didn't stop to eat; he went up to the house and took his dinner back down to the shed with him.

'I'm working on something very important with Glen,' he told his mum and Number Two. 'He's having trouble with his programming facilities,' Ernest lied.

'Is he all right?' his mum asked.

'He'll be fine if I keep at it.'

His mum gave him a sketch, a plan of some sort. 'Could you give Glen this when he's feeling better? It's a new design for the bathroom that I've been working on. I'd like to know what he thinks of it.'

When he went back out, Ernest put his dinner to one side and let it go cold on the bench beside him. There was too much work to do to think about eating. Glen spent most of the night lying down flat on his back with half of his inner central circuitry exposed.

'I hate to be nosy, Ernest,' he asked, 'but what are you doing?'

'I'm bypassing your manual erase unit, and connecting the central receiving recording facilities directly to your ROM units,' Ernest said without looking up.

'Do be careful not to connect my feedback to the output transducer, please, Ernest. I don't know what I'd do if it turned to positive polarity. Possibly explode. Oh dear!'

'Don't worry, I know what I'm doing.'

'Oooh! That tickles. What are you doing now?'

'I'm adapting it to relay frequency.'

'Frequency, what sort of frequency? You won't overload my power bank, will you?'

'I'm putting it through a reducer.'

'Well, that *is* a relief!'

It was nearly ten o'clock when Ernest finally clicked Glen's outer skin back into place. Then he loaded in a cassette, set it on continuous play, and pre-programmed it to the automatic head station to be converted into high-frequency mode.

It was a normal-enough looking tape, but

what it played was something else again.
Ernest had recorded his own voice, on a
carefully designed time sequence, repeating
carefully thought-out phrases such as 'Ernest
is a terrific guy', 'Anything Ernest wants is
okay with me', 'I love Ernest', 'Ernest is a
genius', and, 'I wonder what I can do for
Ernest to make him feel better'.

'I can hear voices,' Glen said, a little dazed
from having been in pieces.

'That's my voice,' Ernest said. 'I've locked
a pre-recorded continuous tape into you. You
can sit up now.'

'It says the same things over and over
again. All about you.'

'You'll get used to it.'

Glen put an arm out for Ernest to take and
help straighten him up.

'My outer sensors don't seem to be picking
it up,' he dithered. 'I'm hearing it on the
inside.'

'I've programmed it to a high frequency.
Nobody will be able to hear it.'

'I can, Ernest.'

'You have to, you're the transmitter.'

'Goodness! You've turned me into a radio!'

'No, you're just transmitting the message on the tape. I've sent it through your automatic frequency selector. It's too high for human ears to pick up. I designed it to penetrate the subconscious mind instead.'

'Do you mean I'm going to be interrupting thought processes? Interfering with human minds!' Glen sounded shocked.

'It's just one more message being sent to the brain,' Ernest shrugged. 'What's one more idea to a brain? Besides, nobody will know it's happening.'

Glen put the back of his hand up against his headpiece and sat down again. 'How am I going to live with myself?'

'I don't know what all the fuss is about,' Ernest said. 'It's not going to hurt anybody.'

'You're going to brainwash people to like you, and I'm going to have to live with it,' Glen went on. 'I won't be able to sleep at night.'

Ernest didn't take any notice. He'd come

too far to stop now.

'I need some data on the range effectiveness of the frequency,' Ernest said. 'Would you please calculate exactly how far the frequency will travel and penetrate the subconscious?'

'No, I won't say.'

'Yes you will!'

'No I won't!'

'Do you want me to break you down into a modular stereo unit?'

'Fifty-one point two metres precisely,' Glen said coldly.

'Good. That should put the house easily within range. I'll go inside and try it out. They should give me anything I want.'

'On your own mother and father!' Glen said disgustedly.

'Just to try it out, that's all,' Ernest said defensively. 'I don't know what you're getting so worked up about.'

Ernest found his mum in the living room. Number Two was too busy to annoy. He was baking scones for an executives' conference the following day. Ernest took a deep breath, walked up to his mum and said, 'I'd like an elephant. Could you pick one up tomorrow?'

His mum looked up from her book with a startled but amused expression. 'I beg your pardon, Ernest?'

'I said I'd like you to pick me up an elephant tomorrow.'

'An elephant?'

'Yes, a real one, of course. You know, tail and trunk and everything.'

'Indian or African?' She was waiting for Ernest to smile. This had to be a joke. 'Is this some sort of game, Ernest?'

'Game? Oh no, I'm quite serious. As a matter of fact, I've never been more serious in my life.'

'You must be tired then. How is Glen?'

'He's okay.'

'I'm pleased to hear that. By the way, isn't it time you went to bed?'

'I'm staying up all night tonight,' Ernest stated flatly.

'Oh you are, are you?' the tone of her voice

was becoming sharp and dangerous.

'Yes, I thought I might,' Ernest said.

'I'm tired, you're obviously tired. It's too late to be playing games, Ernest. It's time you went to bed!'

Something is going wrong. The frequency wasn't working. She was supposed to be agreeing to everything he said.

'Are you sure I can't have an elephant?' he tried once more.

'*Ernest! Go to bed!* You've got five minutes!'

His mum's voice had tightened into anger. Ernest had heard it before; it was time to leave. Five minutes gave him barely enough to get down to the shed and back to the house.

'There's something the matter with it. It didn't work,' Ernest complained to Glen. 'My mum almost bit my head off.'

'I meant to tell you it wouldn't work,' Glen said woodenly.

'Tell me what wouldn't?'

'I'm afraid your pre-recorded message will not have any effect on people if they already like you.'

'Why not?'

'The transmission only works on opposites. It would make no difference to your mum, or Number Two, or anybody who likes you for that matter. It would be rather like telling someone to stand up when they're already standing up. The subconscious rejects it as fact already known. I read it in one of the books.'

'So the more people don't like me, the more effect the frequency will have on them?'

'I'll never be able to face my memory banks again,' Glen agonised to himself.

'It should work *really* well on Rowena then,' Ernest said.

8
Outside interference

A shrill electronic noise sounded from one corner of a small, disused basement. It was a cold, bare room, furnished with a card table, two chairs, and a bench littered with various high technology instruments.

A short, puffy-eyed man in a plain brown suit and loosened tie stood up from his card game and walked across to the source of the noise. It came from a long, oblong-shaped receiver, featureless except for half a dozen dials and a hand-set. He flicked a switch to stop the noise, picked up the hand-set, and spoke into it.

'208.'

Outside interference

'Norman Dern here, 208. Are you alone?'

'262 is here.'

Agent 262 was sitting at the table, looking at a handful of cards. He had on a plain brown suit as well. He was taller and leaner than 208. His most noticeable features were a pair of thin lips and a set of new false teeth behind them. He glanced up at the mention of his code name, then went back to his cards.

'Good,' the voice at the other end crackled. 'I've got a job that requires both of you right now.'

'What about our work here? We've just managed to put a tap on every worthwhile phone in the motel. We're ready to start bringing them in—'

'Drop it!'

'But we've almost got it sewn up here,' Agent 208 protested.

'Don't question my authority!' Norman Dern snapped. 'This is TOP PRIORITY. I'll get somebody else to finish off your job. Right now we need your experience with computer technology. What do you know about frequency output—and tracking it?'

'Enough.'

'Ever heard of the Rockalilly Station?'

'Satellite tracking, weather observation—'

'That's part of it,' Norman Dern interrupted. 'It also engages in certain other activities. Certain very secret activities. It's linked with the Defence Space Program.' There was a short pause at the other end, as if the chief was choosing his words carefully before he spoke. 'They're getting some sort of interference out there. Are you familiar with the CA.123 air traffic scanner?'

'I've seen it.'

'Something, they don't know what or where from, is jamming all their readings on it. All they do know is that it is land-based and somewhere in the country. I shouldn't need to stress the importance, or the danger of this situation.'

'Yes, Sir.'

'I want you to find the source immediately.'

'And then, Sir?'

'Terminate,' he said, 'with extreme

prejudice.'

208 placed the hand-set back into its cradle, then turned to his friend. 'Game's over! Let's pack up, we're wanted elsewhere.'

'Elsewhere! We've spent five days lining this up. We've almost got it sewn up here!' Agent 262 complained.

'Don't question my authority!' 208 snapped. 'This is TOP PRIORITY. We start immediately; we've got some tracking to do.'

Note: While Glen's frequency was effective on human minds only within a radius of fifty-one point two metres, it could affect computers at a greater distance. This explains Glen's interference with the Rockalilly Tracing CA.123 computer.

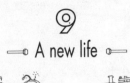

A new life

Ernest and Glen stopped outside Rowena's door the following morning on their way to school. Rowena didn't have a front yard; her door stepped straight out on to the street.

'Well, here goes,' Ernest said.

'Do you mind if I go back home?' Glen said.

'You can't go back home. We're in this together.'

'I'm only here by force, I want you to know that,' Glen said. 'If I had my choice I'd rather be back helping your mum with the new bathroom.'

'Will you stop trying to put me off! I'm

A new life

going to go through with it. Nothing is going to stop me!' Ernest took two steps up to the door and started pounding on it with his fist. 'Hey, Rowena!' he shouted. *'Hurry up and get out here!'*

He paused and listened. He heard a voice say, 'What's that awful racket out there?' It sounded like Rowena's dad. Ernest began pounding again, louder this time.

'Come on, Rowena! I can't wait all day!'

He stopped again after a while. This time he could hear footsteps approaching. The door clicked free and swung open. It was Rowena! She met him with a sneer, a nasty, cruel face poised to attack. Then suddenly her expression changed. She frowned, went blank for a moment, and she was left with a weak, uncertain sort of smile. It grew steadily across her face until her mouth looked like a nasty cut stretched between her nose and chin. Rowena wasn't used to smiling.

'Ernest!' she exclaimed happily. 'I'm sorry if I kept you waiting. Did you want to see me about something?'

'Not particularly,' Ernest said, 'I was just on my way to school so I thought I'd wake you up.' Ernest decided to really test the frequency out. 'Where's your stupid dog?'

"You mean Butch? He's out back somewhere.'

'Best place for him. He's a menace to society, that dog.'

'Yes, I suppose you're right.'

'You two look so much alike I can hardly tell you apart sometimes,' Ernest went on. 'The only way I can tell who's who is that you're the one wearing the clothes.'

'Ha! Hey, you're right! That's funny. I never thought of it like that before.'

Glen made a moaning noise to himself.

'Do you want to carry my bag to school?'

'May I?' Rowena's little eyes lit up.

'Yes, I thought I might let you, if you hurry up.'

'I won't be a second.' Rowena dashed off back down the hall and came back with her own bag. 'Okay, I'm ready,' she said.

They set off for school with Rowena

A new life

carrying the bags. Every so often she would lag behind them and Ernest would have to hurry her up, but she managed to keep up most of the way. Ernest had specially packed his bag full of books. He had books in that bag he would never ever read. He had so many books in that bag he couldn't even do the zip up. But Rowena did have a break along the way when they stopped for an ice cream.

'I'll go in and get it for you,' Rowena offered. 'What would you like?'

'That depends on how much money you've got.'

Rowena pulled a handful of grubby change out of her pocket.

'Eighty-three cents,' she said.

'Something expensive, I think. Nuts and things. A caramel-nut sundae will do.'

'Oh, they cost a lot. I won't get one for myself then.'

'You didn't want one, did you?' Ernest asked.

'No, I don't care. I'm always eating ice creams. I can go without. I'll be right back, so don't go away.'

'I'll never be able to look another machine in the face,' Glen said to no one in particular.

'This is the best day of my life,' Ernest said.

'My terminals are twisting in their sockets with the shame of it.'

Rowena came back with the sundae. 'Here's your ice cream, Ernest.'

'I wanted a drumstick.'

'You did? I thought you said a sundae. I'm sorry, Ernest, I'm so stupid sometimes. I'll change it.'

Ernest made her go back and change it four times, until he finally decided to settle for a Mars Bar.

When they walked in through the front gate at school a startling thing happened. All heads turned to look at Ernest. It was as if a line of trumpeters had heralded his arrival, only there was no sound, no sound that anybody could hear, anyway.

Robert was the first to go over. He stood up from where he was lounging and ran across

A new life

with his hand outstretched. Ernest gave him his hand and let him shake it briefly.

'Hiya' Ernest,' he said. 'We'd started to think you weren't going to come.'

Then Jim Murphy and Greg Jones and Pauline Jenkins got up and came over. In no time at all there was a crowd six deep around Ernest.

'Hi, Ernest!'

'How are you going, Ernest?'

'Morning, Ernest!'

Reg Kennedy, the best footballer in school, grabbed his hand and said, 'Say, Ernest, how about coming over and kicking the footy around for a while, huh? What do you say?'

'I'll think about it, Reg.'

'Sure. Okay, Ernest.'

Doug McCauley said, 'Naw, you don't want to play football. Come over to the nets and we'll do some cricket practice together. That is, if you want to. You can bowl—or bat.'

'Anything we can do for you Ernest?'

'Gee, I feel better now that Ernest is here.'

'Me too.'

'You want a sandwich, Ernest? Pickled tomato, my favourite.'

'Not just now, thanks Greg.'

'How about a cake?' somebody else asked.

'No, let me!' somebody else shouted.

Rex looked up from the taps where he'd been drinking and squinted across at the scene over by the gate. Ernest had barely moved from the gate, which put Rex out of the frequency range by roughly six or seven metres.

'Is that Ernest Pickle over there?' Colin asked beside him.

'That's who it looks like.'

'Hey. They're ganging up on him. Let's go join in,' he added excitedly.

'It looks like they're patting him on the back!' Rex said, in wonderment.

'You're right, it does look like that. Naw, can't be. Are you sure?'

'Maybe he's giving things away again,' Rex suggested. Rex snatched Colin's cricket ball out of his hand. 'You just watch me break them up.'

A new life

Rex wound himself up, pulled his arm back, took aim, and threw the ball, long and fast. (Rex was famous for his long straight throwing. He'd been known to knock the lid off a rubbish bin from seventy-five metres away.) The ball sailed through the air, climbed a little, levelled itself out, and flew straight down into the middle of Ernest's crowd. It hit and made a loud clang that rang across the quadrangle like a dull bell being struck.

'I must have hit a rubbish bin or something,' Rex said, disappointed.

'You must have hit something! Look at the way they're all fussing about,' Colin said.

It took four people to lift Glen back on to his feet again. The cricket ball had sent him over on to his back on the ground like a bowling pin. There was a dent the depth of a dessert bowl in his chest.

'Are you all right?' Ernest asked.

'Am I still operating?' Glen said dizzily.

'Lucky it hit where it couldn't do any damage.'

'I knew something like this was going to

happen,' Glen started once he was back on his feet. 'I should have turned myself off and stayed at home. Flying cricket balls the size of comets! Life was so much simpler when all I had to worry about was a little disc gear. It's ruined my whole body line, I look like an old tin can. Look at the size of this dent. I'll never look the same!'

'I'll straighten you out tonight,' Ernest offered.

'Creased for life,' Glen said, not listening.

'Are you all right, Ernest?' somebody asked, once the crowd had got over its initial shock.

'That almost hit Ernest!'

'Are you okay, Ernest?'

They had forgotten about Glen and were gathering even closer around Ernest.

'Don't worry about me,' Glen said, 'I've just been ruined. Forget about me.'

They had.

'That was Rex,' Rowena muttered under her breath. 'Don't you worry, Ernest, I'll fix him for that. It could've hit you!'

Rex had started to walk over. 'I'll go get your ball back,' he snickered to Colin. 'I'll give Pickle a shove while I'm over there.'

Colin was staying where he was. He felt that something odd was going on. The look on everybody's faces didn't make sense.

A strange feeling passed over Rex. It started off as a small, prodding sensation as he left the taps. It had something to do with Ernest. Maybe he was overdoing it with Ernest. 'What am I thinking?' he asked himself. 'Ernest deserves all that he gets—' No, there was no denying it, he couldn't ignore it. He was experiencing a sensation of warmth towards Ernest, and, worse still, a feeling that he had just done something terribly wrong.

He was suddenly seeing Ernest in a different light. And the closer he got, the more the feeling grew. The way Ernest just stood there, with his hands in his pockets, so relaxed. There was something proud and strong about Ernest. He hadn't even flinched when the ball had almost hit him. That had taken courage. For the first time in his life Rex was seeing Ernest as he really was: a born leader—and a genius.

By the time Rex had reached the little crowd, he couldn't even bear living with the thought that there had actually been a time when he hadn't liked Ernest. And when the crowd parted, and he stood no more than a metre away from Ernest, he felt as if he was shrinking. He was so small and insignificant compared with Ernest, who seemed to be towering above him.

'I'm sorry, Ernest I—' He could hardly speak, he felt so ashamed.

'You could have hit me then, Rex,' Ernest said coldly.

Rex dropped to his knees. 'I don't know what got into me, Ernest, I really don't. I'm such an idiot sometimes. It was—' He started to lie. He had been about to say that Colin had nudged him. But he couldn't lie to Ernest. He just couldn't. Ernest took the last half of his Mars Bar out of his pocket and finished it while he thought about things. He screwed up

A new life

the wrapper and gave it to Rex.

'Put this in the bin for me, will you?'

Ernest made a big show of stretching his arms.

'I might get myself a drink of water now,' he said.

Everybody walked across to the taps with him and watched him drink. When he had finished refreshing himself he had Rex bring him his bag. Then he picked up Rex's bag and threw it up on the toilet roof. Rex stood smiling stupidly. Next Ernest took a length of rope out of his own bag, and handed it to Rex.

'You can go and tie yourself up to one of the toilet doors now.'

'I don't think I can,' Rex said, sorry for himself, 'not by myself. I'd need help.'

'Colin, could you help him?'

'Sure, Ernest.'

As the bell rang and everybody began escorting Ernest into class, one person dawdled along behind. She didn't understand any of this. It was like some sort of play, it couldn't be real. Ernest had never been

Ernest Pickle's Remarkable Robot

popular, but today everybody wanted to be his friend. It didn't make sense, it didn't make any sense at all. 'What's going on?' Elizabeth asked herself.

Rex was bewildered too. The bell had rung, and he'd found himself tied to a toilet door. Everybody had gone inside and he had to get the caretaker to help him down.

'I must have been mad to let that little twerp do this to me,' he growled. 'I'll kill him for this. I'll kill him!'

But Rex would change his mind by the time he got into class.

Mr Carruthers sat up straight when Ernest walked into the classroom. There was something different about Ernest this morning. He seemed to have an air of importance about him. Funny, he hadn't noticed it before. He had been his teacher for almost two years, and it had just this minute dawned on him. It was a privilege to have Ernest in his class. You didn't get many students like Ernest, so naturally intelligent. 'I

A new life

must see what I can do for him,' Mr Carruthers thought to himself. He stood up and said, 'Good morning, Ernest, glad you could come.'

'Morning, Ted,' Ernest said back to him in passing. (Ted was Mr Carruthers' first name.)

Once everyone was sitting down, Mr Carruthers opened up the maths book in front of him and talked about the work they were going to be doing.

'Now, is all that clear?' he asked. 'I want everybody to open up to page 132, and start at Chapter II, on fractions. Then you're to work through page 133, and two thirds of the way down page 134—except for you, Ernest, of course.' He paused. 'Did you have anything particular you wanted to do today, Ernest? Any of your own projects?'

'I thought I might read a couple of magazines,' Ernest said casually.

'Righto. Well, just give me a yell if you get bored, or if you feel like a game of cards or something.'

'This isn't natural,' Elizabeth murmured.

'I'm positive my multi-distributor is

damaged,' Glen said beside her. 'I'm going to need a whole new chest plate put in, that is if Ernest can get me one that lines up properly. There is every possibility that it won't, of course. Machines such as myself are rarely ever the same after an accident, particularly not delicate ones such as myself—'

'What is happening to everybody? Why is everybody acting like Ernest is so special all of a sudden?' Elizabeth asked. She had stopped listening to Glen ages ago, and was looking about the room, staring from face to face. She felt as if she were in somebody else's dream. 'Do I look pale?' she added.

'I'll probably develop a rattle,' Glen went on to himself.

Elizabeth stopped trying to get anything out of Glen. She leaned across the aisle to Greg instead and whispered to him, 'Do I look all right to you?'

Greg shrugged. 'I guess so.'

'Does anything about Ernest seem odd to you, the way everybody is acting towards him?'

A new life

'Odd? No.'

One of Ernest's magazines slid off his desk and on to the floor. Rex got up out of his seat, walked down the aisle, and picked it up for him. 'You dropped this, Ernie,' he said.

Ernest hated being called Ernie, but he accepted the magazine anyway. Elizabeth shook her head from side to side.

'Rex hates Ernest. I've seen him try to kill Ernest every day for the last two years!'

Greg shrugged again.

'Anybody would think it was Burt Reynolds sitting there instead of Ernest Pickle.'

Greg glared at her. 'That's a poor joke, Elizabeth.'

'But Ernest just isn't that popular.'

'Are you saying that you don't *like* Ernest?'

It was useless trying to get any sense out of Greg. She tried Sandra behind her.

'Remember that time you drew that sketch of Ernest and made him look like a pipe cleaner—'

'I've been trying to forget it all morning,'

Ernest Pickle's Remarkable Robot

Sandra said.

'—and I snatched it from you and said it was a dirty thing to do?' Elizabeth paused to think, then added, 'That really happened, didn't it? And it *was* you who said Ernest reminded you of a lizard, wasn't it?'

'I was younger then,' Sandra said. 'I've come to realise certain things about Ernest that I didn't realise before. I think he is the most wonderful, thoughtful, exciting human being I know.'

'Somebody must have slipped something into my orange juice this morning. It all seems strange, or maybe it's just me.'

'I'm sure it's just you,' Sandra said. 'There's nothing to worry about. Ernest has changed, that's all. Maybe you're just a little slow to recognise it. Just go with the flow.'

'I suppose you could be right.'

Elizabeth had some trouble going with the flow. However, she went along with it when he was voted school captain at lunch time. Ernest was very sensible and would probably handle responsibility well. But then he was unanimously elected cricket, football, and volleyball captain, and Ernest was hopeless at sport. After that he was nominated for band master, head monitor, and given honorary membership of the school swimming team. (Ernest couldn't swim.)

Elizabeth tried to go with the flow, but it got worse. She tried patting him on the back and chanting his name with everybody else, but it just didn't feel right. And besides, it gave her a sick feeling in her stomach. She knew she liked him. 'Maybe I just don't like him as much as I thought I did,' she wondered to herself. 'I can't, or else I'd be with everybody else.' Elizabeth took to running around the oval instead. 'And Rowena's the worst,' she panted to herself. 'I've never seen her like anybody in such a way before.'

There was no doubt that Rowena was Ernest's most devoted fan. She proposed all the motions to have him elected, brushed down seats for him, turned on taps, opened all his doors, peeled all his fruit (and not very well). She unwrapped his lunch, handled his public affairs, brushed his hair whenever it got out of place (which Ernest hated). She never left his side, not for a moment. She even tried to sit on his knee and he had to tell her NO!

'It's like having a manager,' Ernest grumbled to Glen.

Rex was the second most devoted fan of Ernest's, then Colin, Jim Murphy, Pauline, Greg, Robert, etc.; they stayed by his side as if they were glued to him. When they walked him home they wouldn't leave, and after three hours Ernest's mum had to order them to go.

10

Goodnight

'**W**ell, they've finally gone home,' Ernest said sleepily to Glen.

He was in bed, leaning over looking down at Glen who was sleeping on the floor. He said he preferred it that way. He didn't want to sleep in the same bed as a dictator.

'You know,' Ernest went on, 'there are certain problems with the frequency I never counted on: all these people. Everywhere I go there are people with me. All I did today was sign autographs. I didn't mind the first five or six, but there was no end to them.' He paused and thought for a moment. 'Yep, I'll have to put a stop to the autographs.'

'I'm ridden with guilt!' Glen cried into his pillow.

'And Rowena, she never leaves me alone. I couldn't even put my hand in my pocket today without her wanting to know what I was doing. I wanted to go across and talk to Elizabeth, but Rowena was always there. I'm pretty sure Elizabeth will be impressed now that I've got so many friends. If only they would leave me alone sometimes. Especially Rowena. I mean, it's not as if I like her all that much, not to hang around with every minute of the day, anyway. I just wanted her to like me, I didn't know she'd attach herself to me. She's almost as annoying as she used to be when she hated me. I never counted on that. Not that I'm complaining or anything; I'm still having a great time.' He paused again. 'It's just that there are one or two things I never figured on.'

'I hate to trouble you, Ernest, but would you mind turning me off? I can't sleep. My solar circuitry is keeping me awake.'

Ernest leant across further and switched

Glen off, except for the frequency which was programmed on automatic.

Ernest felt like talking more. He lay there for a long time listening to the night sounds. He thought about turning Glen back on. Glen would have to listen to him, of course, if he did. But he changed his mind and decided to leave him off. He didn't think he would enjoy talking as much if Glen didn't really want to listen.

It was quiet without Glen.

11

The Ernest Pickle fund

Ernest took his party invitations to school the following morning. Two hundred of them. There was a lot of excitement about them, particularly since there were four hundred at school. That meant that half were going to miss out. Ernest's party invitations were to fetch up to ten dollars a piece on the shelter-shed black market in the days that followed.

Doug Jeffries sold his to a pair of fully-grown men down by the side gate for fifteen dollars. He didn't bother asking them what they wanted them for, and they didn't ask who else was going to the party, or even what it was for. They knew it had something to do with

Ernest Pickle, and they knew Ernest Pickle had something to do with why they were there. The tall one with the new teeth simply put the invitation in a pocket of his brown suit, and paid Doug the money.

The other exciting development was THE ERNEST PICKLE FAN CLUB. Rowena was the founding member: she wrote the rules. Those who wanted to join had to pay two dollars and pledge loyalty and constant friendship to Ernest. Each paying member was then given a certificate with a number on it, and a photo of Ernest Relaxing At Home to carry around in their back pockets or hang around their necks. The joining fee of two dollars was put into THE ERNEST PICKLE FUTURE FUND which had never had the chance to amount to anything because most of the money was used up to replace photos that members would throw away once they got home and out of the frequency range.

There was also an ERNEST PICKLE CHANT which had to be memorised before entrance to the club was cleared.

It went:

Who's the number one we love?

Who's the number one we adore?

Who's the one who stands above us all?

Who's the opposite to being a bore?

ERNEST! ERNEST! ERNEST!

Who makes our life so swell?

Who makes us feel all right?

Who makes the party jell?

Who's the one who's always right?

IT'S ERNEST! ERNEST! ERNEST!

It went on in this tedious fashion for twenty-four verses. Rowena had written it, of course.

'It all sounds the same,' Glen said. 'It's worse than listening to readout tape.'

Even Ernest got sick of hearing it after a while. Rowena made everybody recite it in front of him for his approval. 'I wouldn't mind if it was just five or six verses,' Ernest said to Glen, 'but it just goes on and on and on!'

Soon practically everybody in school was a member of the club—except for Elizabeth. She had begun to spend a lot of time by herself. When she wasn't lapping the oval, she would sit somewhere quiet and read. She found it was absolutely hopeless trying to have a conversation with her friends because they only wanted to talk about Ernest. However, Elizabeth didn't bother even saying hello to him any more. Whenever she saw him coming, she would make a point of looking the other way. He seemed to be ignoring her, anyway. Besides, she didn't like cult figures. She'd read somewhere that they had deep psychological problems.

Ernest wasn't really ignoring Elizabeth at all; he watched her every time he got a chance, usually from a distance. There were always so many heads in the way, mostly belonging to people crowded around him. And if it wasn't that, there was always somebody pestering him, asking him if he was okay, or if there was anything they could do for him. And being captain and honorary member of so many things took up a lot of his time, too. There were always meetings people wanted him to attend and talk at. Then there was Rowena, who was writing his biography. He couldn't speak without her asking him to repeat it, so that she could get it down in full. Reg Kennedy was always wanting him to play football, too. Ernest didn't like football, and he didn't think much of Reg Kennedy either; he was always looking at himself in the locker-room mirror. Then there was Rex, always calling him *Ernie*. No matter how many times Ernest reminded him, he kept on forgetting and calling him by that name, and in public as well.

'I'm sorry, Ernie, whoops, I mean *Ernest*. I can't help it, I always have pet names for my friends.'

As the days dragged by, Ernest became more of a success and more sought after. He was getting fan mail by the bag. Many people wrote asking for his thoughts on life.

'I can't afford the stamps,' Ernest said, troubled.

The headmaster started inviting him in to his office for afternoon tea.

'He's boring and his office smells like

The Ernest Pickle fund

mothballs,' Ernest complained.

His teacher, Mr Carruthers, wouldn't leave him alone in class. He was always asking him what he thought about his teaching. 'Do you think I was too harsh? Do you think I was getting across to everyone today? Do you think the lesson was interesting?'

There was no end to it. Ernest's name was entered in sporting events he didn't particularly want to go in. Everybody wanted him to be on their team. He became the best footballer the school had had in twenty-eight years; he kicked eighty-three goals in one match alone (not bad for someone who had to keep on asking which end he was kicking towards). The other players, on both sides, stood out of his way whenever the ball went near him, or else went out of their way, sometimes running as far as fifty metres, to hand him the ball personally.

'I don't feel like the best footballer in twenty-eight years,' Ernest said.

He was virtually unbowlable in cricket. Everybody insisted on bowling underarm to him. He usually retired from boredom.

In basketball he was given so many free shots it was hard to tell if there was an opposing team at all.

'Great game, Ernest!' The players stood around congratulating him afterwards.

'Top score!'

'I've never seen anything like it!'

'Did you see the way he put that last basket in?'

'I didn't think he was going to do it for a while there.'

'Aw, I knew he was going to make it all along.'

'Oh yeah, what makes you think you know Ernest any better than me?'

'I do, I've know him longer. Haven't I, Ernest?'

'Don't bother Ernest!'

'I'm not bothering him. Am I bothering you, Ernest?'

Ernest wasn't interested. They were *all* bothering him. Voices. They were all just nagging little voices to him. They all sounded the same. Even their faces seemed to blend together and were beginning to look like one another. He couldn't concentrate on them. He could barely tell them apart, there were so many of them. More than that, they all seemed to be saying the same things, over and over again.

It was Elizabeth he was thinking of. She was different, he knew it. He could see her sitting over by one of the gum trees by herself, reading a book. He decided to slip away and go over and talk to her. He even left Glen behind with the group. They were so absorbed in arguing amongst themselves they wouldn't notice he'd left for a while. Rowena wasn't there for a change, either. She'd been forced to leave him and go off and play rounders.

Ernest sneaked away to his bag and took out the special invitation he'd been saving for Elizabeth. He'd coloured it in himself and put it in a brown envelope to keep it clean. Then he walked over to where she was.

'Hi, Elizabeth. I brought you over this.' Ernest handed the envelope to her and almost sat down. Elizabeth looked up from her book. She was reading *Outline of Psychoanalysis*, by Sigmund Freud. She stared down at the envelope for a moment, opened it, glanced inside, and closed it again.

'Thanks, but no thanks.'

Ernest's heart sank to the soles of his sandals. He'd almost forgotten what it felt like to be rejected, and it felt even worse coming from Elizabeth.

'I coloured it in myself,' he said shyly.

'Oh.' Elizabeth pretended to go back to reading her book.

'I've invited practically everybody from school.'

'Oh.'

There was no doubt that Elizabeth wasn't affected by the frequency. 'At least she still likes me a little, anyway,' Ernest thought, trying to console himself.

'Interesting book?' Ernest asked. Elizabeth nodded. He was going to have to try a bit harder. 'I'm reading a book called *Subconscious Thought Transferral* at the moment. It's very interesting.'

'Oh.'

'It discusses some of Freud's theories. It mainly deals with hypnotism and subliminal suggestion and that sort of—' Ernest suddenly stopped. What was he doing, talking about subliminal suggestion? He couldn't afford to have anyone suspect, even for a moment, that he knew anything about that subject. Elizabeth wasn't looking at her book any more. She was staring at Ernest with a quizzical expression on her face.

'And what else?'

'Nothing. I haven't read any further. That's as far as I've got.'

'They used to use subliminal suggestion in advertising, to affect people's subconscious minds, didn't they?'

'I don't know, did they?'

'Sure, I remember now. My brother was telling me about it.' Elizabeth sat up excited. 'They used it at drive-ins. I remember because my brother could never figure out why he always got hungry just before interval. It was because they slipped in photos of chips and hamburgers every sixteen frames or so. Too fast for the eye, but just enough for the subconscious to see them. There was a big fuss about it too—'

There was a yell from across the yard. Somebody had spotted Ernest. A group of devotees swarmed on them before Elizabeth could finish her sentence.

'Say, where have you been, Ernest?'

'We've been looking everywhere for you.'

Ernest looked around to see where Elizabeth was, but she had disappeared. He slumped down on the bench.

'You don't look so hot, Ernie, something on your mind?'

'Why don't you try lying down for a while?'

'I bet it was that girl Elizabeth!' somebody said. 'I saw her talking to Ernest before, just as we came along.'

'She must have upset him. She's not a club member either, is she?'

'Come to think of it,' Greg said, 'she was

asking me some might funny questions about Ernest the other day.'

'Me too!' Sandra piped up.

Ernest was trying not to listen, but their voices felt like sharp sticks, poking and prodding him.

'How about a walk, Ernest?'

'Yes, a walk would be nice,' Ernest said slowly. He felt giddy.

'Right. Where will we go?'

'I want to go alone,' Ernest said.

'Are you sure?'

'Will you be safe?'

'We'd better go with you, just in case—'

'Stay here!' Ernest snapped. 'I want to go for a walk by myself for once. You never leave me alone! You're like flies buzzing around me all the time. I don't want any of you to walk with me, eat lunch with me, walk over to the taps with me, walk over to the library with me. I don't want any of you to go anywhere with me any more, ever!'

There was a brief silence, then, 'We'll wait here for you, Ernest.'

'Coming, Glen?'

'Do I have to?'

'Why not? What else are you going to do?'

'I thought I might stay here, with everybody else.'

'Stay here! With everybody else?'

'We have been seeing a lot of each other lately. I thought it might be nice to have a break.'

'Now you're turning against me,' Ernest said miserably. 'What's wrong, Glen, you've changed.'

'Machines do not have the capacity for change. It is only humans who can change.'

'Well, I haven't changed. I order you to come with me!'

They walked together down around the oval, but there were only more fans out there. Ernest and Glen had to hide in the boys' shower block to get away from everybody. It was the only place where he knew he wouldn't bump into anybody and Rowena couldn't follow him.

'Couldn't you have picked somewhere a

little drier?' Glen complained.

They were standing side by side, huddled together in one of the shower cubicles. There was a lot of water dropping down between them. The shower block was known for its leaky taps. The caretaker always had a lot of trouble with washers as he had a habit of putting them in the wrong way around.

'This can't be what it's like to have friends,' Ernest moaned.

'Does that mean you're going to turn my frequency off?'

'I didn't say that.'

'How long can I go on living with this shame?'

'It's just a bit much for me right now. I'm not used to having so many friends. I just have to learn to adapt. Sure, there are a few annoying bits about it, like having people hanging around who you don't like very much. But I'll learn to live with it, I suppose, eventually.' Ernest went on talking to himself. 'Maybe there's some sort of night course I can do, on how to handle new friends. I'll have to look into it.'

A drop of water splashed down on Glen's head. He moved along, further in. 'Heaven knows I was not built for these damp conditions. I can feel moisture collecting on my circuits already.'

'You're waterproof.'

'I'll probably seize up and have to be carried out of here. Being waterproof and having a shower are two different things. There is every chance I could arc and short any moment.'

'You worry too much,' Ernest said.

Another drop fell on Glen's head, and rolled quickly down over his metal chest (the one with the dent in it).

'Well, somebody has to worry about me. I am a delicate piece of equipment, after all. Some people would think so, anyway. I wasn't built for standing about on concrete floors in puddles. Personally I wouldn't treat a pocket calculator like this. Machines aren't like people, they need—'

The Ernest Pickle fund

Glen went on complaining until the bell rang and they could sneak back into class.

12

The rescue: part one

Ernest kept to himself during the afternoon. He sat through the science lesson browsing through his computer magazines. He didn't read them, he just looked. He'd already read them the day before, but there was nothing else he could think of that he particularly wanted to do. He glanced over at Elizabeth from time to time, but she didn't look back.

He still had afternoon recess to get through. He still didn't feel like adapting to his new friends, but there was always the boys' shower block. It wasn't much of a way to spend afternoon recess, but it was better than being harassed to death. When the bell rang, and

The rescue: part one

everybody poured out into the yard, Ernest and Glen sneaked away, back to the leaky cubicle.

The dripping water must have been getting louder because by the time they stepped back out into the playground, it was deserted. They had missed the bell.

'We can't have missed it by much,' Ernest said.

'Another minute in that place and I would have been wet up to my tapes,' Glen complained.

'They started off across the quadrangle but were stopped by a cry.

'*Help!* Can anybody hear me? Somebody, anybody! Help!'

'I detect that it was coming from the shelter shed,' Glen said.

They hurried back in the direction they had come from, past the shower block, on across the basketball courts and into the shelter shed. The sight of Mr Carruthers' legs poking and waving down through the roof of the shed was the last thing Ernest expected to see.

'Help! Quick, help!'

Ernest and Glen ran around to the outside to see the other half of him sticking out from the waist up. At that moment Elizabeth rounded the corner. She had been running around the oval and had missed the bell too.

'What's happened?'

'I think he's trying to kill himself,' Ernest said.

'Don't be silly, he wouldn't be calling for help.'

'Maybe he changed his mind.'

'What are you doing up there, Mr Carruthers?' Elizabeth called out.

'Trying not to fall. I got up here to get whatsisname's stupid football down for him, and it just caved in!' Mr Carruthers looked hot and excited. 'Well, don't just stand there, please! Go and get help. I can feel the roof giving way!'

'I'll go!' Elizabeth called out. She could run for hours if she had to.

'I'll stay then, will I?' Ernest said. 'I'll keep him company.'

But Elizabeth wasn't there to answer him as she had already set off for the main building. Suddenly there was the sound of wood splintering, coming from inside.

'It's going!' Mr Carruthers shouted. 'It's going!'

Ernest and Glen ran back around inside the shed. Half a beam had broken free and crashed to the floor.

'I'm falling! I can't hold on any longer.'

'Try to hang on!' Ernest shouted from below.

'I'm falling! It's going! Watch out down *thereeeee*!'

That Glen happened to spring forward and catch Mr Carruthers in his arms was due to the split-second calculations of his data processing capabilities. That he collapsed from the weight, and finished up sprawled out flat underneath Mr Carruthers, was probably due to Ernest's miscalculations. He hadn't built Glen with the requirements necessary for catching people dropping from great heights.

⟜∘ The rescue: part two ∘⟝

Mr Carruthers was still out cold by the time Elizabeth came back with help—if you could call the headmaster 'help'. He dithered and fussed around so much Elizabeth had to run off again to find somebody else to help the headmaster.

Mr Carruthers came around eventually. He couldn't seem to recall what had happened. The last thing he remembered was putting a leg through the roof.

Everybody wanted to know how Ernest had rescued him, of course. Well, it had to be Ernest. There hadn't been anybody else there except for Ernest and his contraption. And it

The rescue: part two

was obvious Mr Carruthers couldn't have survived a drop from that height if he'd fallen by himself. It occurred to Ernest to tell the truth, but it just would have made things too complicated. How was he going to explain that a robot ran across and caught a fully-grown man in his metal arms? And what if it got in the newspapers? Ernest decided to lie instead.

He went into careful detail about how he'd climbed up the ladder, stepped up on the roof and skilfully lassoed Mr Carruthers under the armpits with his rope. Then he'd slowly lowered him to the ground, until he was sure Mr Carruthers had made it down safely.

'Funny, I don't remember a thing,' Mr Carruthers said for the sixty-fifth time that afternoon. 'I must have blacked out.'

Glen has suffered two more dents: a crease in his left hip, and a rather nasty bash to his left shoulder plate. His speech facilities were slightly damaged as well. His s's came out sounding like r's.

'At least the frequency isn't damaged,' Ernest commented, looking him over later in the day. 'That's a relief.'

'I'm rurprired I can rtill rtand up. Look at me: barhed from head to foot. I look like an old rtock car.'

'Don't panic, I can fix that.' Ernest had a screwdriver out and was re-adjusting Glen's speech tuning. 'In the meantime, I'll just repair your oral relays.'

'I don't know why I even bothered. I didn't even get the credit, not that I need public acclaim, of courre. But a little rympathy-wtyufgmdfe ... would be akkceptable, and xome thangs would have— jjuifxxzmsssuipoilll ... been appreciated. Now I tan't even sunderstandy what I'm taying any more. Life isn't worth living.'

13
⊸ Ernest's clear head ⊸

Ernest's popularity soared to even greater heights. The following day the headmaster called a school assembly to honour what he called 'Ernest's bravery under extreme circumstances'. It dragged on for hours.

First the headmaster gave a speech about what a fine student Ernest was, and how he was an excellent representative of the school spirit. Then the deputy headmaster stood up and said more or less the same things. Then Mr Carruthers got up and said a few hundred thousand words about the events leading up to the accident. Then finally Ernest himself gave a talk entitled:

Keeping A Clear Head
In Life And Death Situations.

His mum and Number Two had been invited to the assembly. They sat on the platform behind Ernest. Number Two slept through most of it because he's been working fourteen hours a day organising Ernest's party. There was a lot that had to be done for two hundred guests. He only woke up in the clapping between speeches long enough to clap the next guest, and then fall back asleep.

On the roof of the boys' toilets, lying down between channels, were two spectators who were anything but sleepy. They were interested in what everybody had to say, particular Ernest.

They were serious-faced men, both in plain brown suits (standard ISIO dress). The shorter and heavier of the two, known as agent 208, pulled a plastic-cased compact receiver out of the inside pocket of his jacket and called in.

'208 here.'

'Reading you,' Norman Dern's voice crackled back.

'We've sourced the interference. We're at a school called West Wood, east of the city.'

'Exact position?'

'We've traced it to a student here named Ernest Pickle.'

'I'll run a check on him.'

'We don't know what it is, or how he does it, but he's our boy, all right. Our indicators show the source is on him. Wherever he goes the signal goes—loud and clear.'

'Are you positive it's him?'

'Absolutely, Sir. From the information we've gathered he's some sort of a whiz-kid. He's always fiddling about with computers.'

'Anything else?'

'He's very popular with the other students. Apart from that, nothing.'

'Proceed, then.'

'What about the kid?'

'You'll use some discretion. After all, we're not murderers. But just as importantly, do whatever is necessary. Whatever it is he's playing around with has to be put out of operation, and fast. I suggest you terminate it, but drop him back home.'

'Yes, Sir.'

The ISIO agent zipped the receiver back into its plastic case and returned it to his pocket.

'Let's move,' he said to his partner.

Ernest's talk went on almost as long as Mr Carruthers' not only because it was so long, but also because he kept on forgetting what he was talking about, and had to keep referring to his notes. Elizabeth was the only person in the school not listening. She had managed to sneak off without any of the teachers noticing. Glen was standing, partially hidden, down behind the school hall. Elizabeth spotted him shimmering in the sun and went around to talk to him.

'That's a nasty bash on your shoulder, Glen.'

'There is more. Down on my hip, for example—'

'There's something bothering me,' Elizabeth started. She didn't have much time for sick people, but apart from that she was a nice person. 'It's the rescue. It doesn't add up. I've been figuring it out, mathematically and everything, and I've come to the conclusion that Ernest *couldn't* have rescued Mr Carruthers.'

'It would have needed to be someone extremely quick-witted,' Glen suggested.

'And besides that,' Elizabeth continued, 'how could skinny Ernest lower somebody as big as Mr Carruthers down on a rope?'

'Highly unlikely,' Glen agreed.

'And what about the rope? Where was the rope? I was there before and after, and I didn't see any rope.'

'Neither did I.'

'But what confuses me the most is why nobody else has noticed. It's obvious Ernest couldn't have done it. So why doesn't anybody else notice?'

Glen remained silent.

'Nobody around this place seems to *think*

any more. Anybody would think they're all walking about in a trance, hypnotised or something—'

Elizabeth paused mid-sentence. She remembered the conversation with Ernest the day before. What was that book he'd started talking about? Something to do with hypnotism and subliminal suggestion ... 'It's as if everybody has been hypnotised,' she said to herself again, in a quiet tone this time, as if she was getting used to some new words. 'Yes, it's as if everybody has been hypnotised,' she repeated, louder.

'Oh dear.'

'That's it, isn't it? Ernest has learnt how to hypnotise people, hundreds at a time, so they'll act funny. And you know something about it.'

'I'm afraid I—'

'And I bet he didn't rescue Mr Carruthers either—you did! Yes, of course, that's why you're damaged. Well, you may as well tell me now that I know most of it.'

'If only I could—'

'You've got to!'

'Oh, I wish I could. What a relief it would be to get it off my dented chest. The guilt I've been bearing! But I don't know if I—'

'Please, Glen, for Ernest's sake, not mine. He's turning into a creep.'

Glen paused. He listened to Ernest's voice echoing out of the public address system and around the school grounds. 'I acted on instincts,' he was saying. 'It's surprising what some people can do acting on such instincts. Take my own, for example ...'

'All right, I will,' Glen said. 'The whole story.'

Glen told Elizabeth everything. It took twenty-five minutes, nearly half as long as Ernest's speech. He told her about the party, the books, the frequency range and the effect it had on people, the pre-recorded tape, why it had no effect on Elizabeth herself, and the true story about the rescue.

Elizabeth remained solemn throughout, interrupting every so often with a 'So that's why', or, 'Now it makes sense'. Finally Glen finished, and she stood staring at nothing in particular, speechless.

She went on standing there a full five minutes after Glen had left to go with Ernest after the assembly had broken up. It was the most incredible, unbelievable story she had ever heard, and yet she had to believe it. It all made sense now. She didn't know how Ernest had managed to do it. 'I'll have to stop him,' she said quietly to herself. 'Yep, it's all up to me.'

14

The long way there

The school was given a holiday for the rest of the afternoon. And to celebrate Ernest's great deed, he and the other sixth grades were to be taken to Luna Park (an amusement centre).

Mr Carruthers was out by the front gate trying to organise everybody into lines when Ernest and Glen made their appearance. A great roaring cheer rose from the crowd upon their arrival. Ernest felt terrible. 'I think I'm getting the flu,' he mumbled. He couldn't manage a smile or even a small wave to his fans. 'I'd rather be at home,' he added. He felt worn out. He was tired of crowds and people wanting to get close to him all the time.

'Then you'll switch the frequency off?' Glen said hopefully.

'I didn't say that.'

Mr Carruthers felt sick too, but for different reasons. 'I wish we'd had more time to organise this,' he was complaining to the teacher beside him. 'Everybody wants to go. I don't know who belongs in my class and who is from Ms Dupont's class. I've got kids wandering off looking for stragglers and more kids off looking for the kids looking for stragglers. Luna Park closes in an hour and a half, it looks like it's going to rain, the petty cash is missing, and for some reason we've now got three buses instead of two. We only ordered two. We should have waited till tomorrow. I don't know why we had to rush and do it this afternoon. The whole thing is a disaster!'

'I'll go in the small bus,' Ernest told Mr Carruthers.

'Righto, Ernest.'

'I'd rather travel alone.'

Of course that was impossible. Rowena

took charge of filling the other seven seats in the mini-bus. She gave the honour of riding in the same bus as Ernest only to the most devoted members of the club: Rowena herself, Rex, Colin, Robert, Gary and Pauline. Elizabeth pushed her way on and filled the last spot. Mr Carruthers was supposed to fit in as well, but there was no room, so the bus driver shut the door and set off.

Elizabeth sat quietly looking out the window watching the suburbs slip by, listening to the others talk amongst themselves (always about Ernest). When she had thought about what she had to say, she leaned over to the seat in front where Ernest was, and spoke in his ear alone.

'Phoney.'

Ernest felt a shiver run up his backbone.

'I know what's going on,' Elizabeth added. 'I know about the frequency and the taped message. Glen told me the whole story.'

'I'm sorry, Elizabeth, did you say something?' His voice was trembling.

'At first I figured it was me. I thought *I* was

turning anti-social, but I never imagined, I never would have believed, that you, Ernest Pickle, would resort to such low trick—*brain-washing*!'

Ernest cleared his throat. 'You shouldn't listen to Glen, he exaggerates. I programmed him to.'

'It's too late, Ernest, I don't believe you any more.'

A small, poisonous arrow shot into his heart.

'I'm just popular,' he managed to say. 'I can't help it if it looks suspicious. People just naturally like me.'

'You're not fooling me, Ernest. You know you haven't got all that many friends. Rowena could never like you, not in a thousand years. But then Rowena doesn't like anybody. However,' Elizabeth paused to take a nervous breath, 'I do.'

Ernest began to feel a little better.

'At least I thought I did. I'm not so positive now.'

Ernest started to feel bad again.

'Rex and Colin and Rowena and the others aren't real friends. They never will be,' Elizabeth went on, 'and if you don't stop this I'll stop liking you, and your mum and Number Two will stop liking you. Then you won't have any "real" friends at all.'

The thought of Elizabeth and Number Two and his mum becoming members of his fan club, chanting and following him around like all the rest, threw him into a state of panic.

'No, no! Don't stop liking me, Elizabeth, please!'

'Turn the frequency off, Ernest.'

'All right, I promise. Straight after my party.'

'That's too late. It has to be now.'

'Just a few more days?'

Elizabeth shook her head.

'But I can't do it now. It will take time to deprogram Glen and I haven't got any tools.'

'There must be a way of switching him off now. This is the best time to do it. You can face the worst of them straight away and get it over and done with.'

'I suppose I could disconnect his main power bank,' Ernest said, 'but that would turn him off altogether, and it would take a long time to re-program him.'

'You have to do it, Ernest.'

Ernest leaned across to Glen to make the disconnection, then stopped halfway.

'Couldn't we wait until we were out of the bus? If I have to face Rex and Rowena and Colin and everybody in here, I may not survive.'

'You've got to be brave, Ernest.'

Ernest leaned over to Glen again, but he didn't look very happy about it. He looked as though—

Suddenly the bus lurched to a stop, and the driver switched off the motor. Ernest looked outside. This wasn't Luna Park. They were parked in a narrow street. Either side of the bus were row after row of dull, drab factories: old warehouses with boarded-up doors and windows that didn't look like they'd been used for a long time. The street was dirty and empty except for an old truck parked ahead in the distance. It looked lonely and discarded.

The driver got up from his seat and took off his grey bus-driver's coat. Underneath it he had on a crumpled dark brown suit. He opened the bus door and the other ISIO agent stepped on. He had appeared from a doorway in one of the buildings outside. They both stood facing the group.

'Okay, everybody off!' the driver ordered. His thin lips parted in an unpleasant smile, and his sparkling set of new false teeth shone out. 'We're making a refreshments stop.'

Elizabeth looked at the doorway the second agent had stepped from and said, 'It doesn't look like a refreshments stop.'

'It's nicer inside,' the second one answered roughly. 'Come on, everybody out. In single file!'

'Shove off!' Rowena said. 'We're not stopping for any refreshments.'

'Yeah, come on! Hurry up, we're late already!' Rex called out from the back.

The driver took a gun from his jacket pocket and pointed it in the direction of the group and said, 'We just want to have a little talk, then you can all be on your way again. Now either you can be good kids and walk in, or we're going to have to carry you in.'

'My sensors compute danger,' Glen said.

One of the crumpled suits took a step forward. 'Who said that?'

"The kid in the funny suit over there,' his friend said, pointing.

'What did you say?' the first one asked Glen.

'On which occasion?'

'Just now. What did you say just now?'

'My sensors compute danger. Indeed, apart from your hostile body language, I believe the gun in your hand, which is a—'

'Hold it!' the driver said excitedly, and walked down the aisle and rapped Glen's head with his knuckles. 'He's metal!'

'Do you mind! I am not a front door. Just a simple little tap—'

The agent rapped him across the chest. 'He's all metal! This is no kid in a suit! He's some sort of mechanical man. A robot! He's the gadget!'

'Is this your gadget, kid?'

Ernest didn't answer.

'He has to be!'

'Glen, do something,' Ernest whispered next to him. 'The heat.'

Glen lifted a hand and pointed it at the agent closest. A hot white beam of searing heat the diameter of a broom handle and half as long shot out from his fingers. It caught a corner of the ISIO agent's jacket, and a burst of flame shot from it. The agent leapt back shouting, patting the fire out with his handkerchief. He managed to smother it till all that was left was a smoking, charred patch.

'He tried to set fire to me, Jack!'

Jack, still holding the gun, took a small, black plastic object from one of his pockets, pulled an aerial out from it, and switched a nob around to a pre-set number. He pointed it at Glen. The beam shrank, and died. Glen was left with a warm hand.

'One more stupid move like that and I'll defuse your friend altogether,' he warned

Ernest.

'How did you do that?' Ernest asked, stunned.

'Just a little manual disrupting device. It cancels signals; simple, but effective.'

Ernest looked to see if Glen's frequency had broken down too, but there was no sign that it had. Everybody still looked friendly. Apparently it could jam the manual mode, but it had no effect on fixed, automatic programs. But why weren't these men affected by the frequency? The only answer was that they felt nothing for Ernest one way or another. They had never met him before, so how could they?

'Okay, up!' the new teeth ordered. 'Everybody inside. Now!'

With Glen rendered helpless there was nothing else to do. Elizabeth stood up, then Ernest, then the others followed.

'Just behave yourselves, and you'll all be back home in time for dinner tonight,' the singed agent said.

'You don't seem to realise who Ernest is,' Rowena told him.

'You're right there, kid, we don't.'

'You shouldn't be pushing him around like this,' Rex said. 'He's a very important person.'

'He's not like us,' Colin added.

'What is it with these kids? They're creepy about this Ernest.'

With Elizabeth leading, they got off the bus and entered the doorway. Ahead stretched a dark, dusty corridor. At the far end of it a single dull light globe was burning.

'Post-war designed, I'd say at a glance,' Glen commented to himself as he looked around the corridor.

The agent closest to them told them to keep on walking, in single file, towards the light. On either side of the corridor were small rooms. Most of them had windows smashed in, or doors hanging off. They looked like they had once been offices. The place had a damp, stale smell and their shoes crunched on glass fragments underneath as they continued along.

They reached the end where the globe hung, followed the passage-way around to the right a few steps, then left and into an open, square room. It was just as grubby and wasted-looking as the corridor. It was brightly lit by a fluorescent tube.

In the centre of the room, where the light was concentrated, was a couch, like a doctor's couch, with a clean white sheet thrown over it. The rest of the room, apart from one or two old wooden chairs and some cardboard boxes, was bare. On the right-hand wall were two doors, side by side. They were both closed. The agent with the gun led the way over to the first door on the right and opened it, wide.

'Where are the refreshments?' Colin asked.

'Shut up and get in here!'

He gave Colin a shove, held Ernest to one side, and motioned the others to follow Colin in. Once they were all in, he slammed the door shut and shot a bolt across, locking it.

'What do you want with us?' Ernest asked.

The agent who had been holding on to Glen let him go and stepped over beside the couch.

'We want to ask you one or two questions,' he said.

'About your robot here,' the other one

added.

Ernest's clothes were sticking to him. It was the sweat. 'What about?' he said, trying to sound brave.

'He's interfering with some very important operations.'

'What kind of operations?'

'Never mind that. You've got him throwing out some weird type of frequency and we want to know how you're doing it.'

'And how we stop it.'

'Who are you?'

'We ask the questions here.'

'What's the frequency selection?'

'What's the middle range?'

'I'm not saying anything until you tell me who you are,' Ernest said.

'Make it easy for yourself, kid. Just answer our questions, and you can go.'

'What about Glen?'

'We'll keep the robot here with us.'

'No!'

'Do as they say, Ernest,' Glen said, 'I'll be all right. The worst they can do is torture me.

Forget about me, Ernest, save yourself. I can stand it—I suppose.'

'The machine's talking sense, Ernest. Tell us what we want to know.'

'Tell Number Two,' Glen went on, 'to link the battery condenser through the plastic core of his toothbrush. That should enable him to alter the size of the speaker and he can move it further along the handle. And remind your mum that if she puts the window in the southern wall and extends into the laundry, there may be some trouble—'

'What's he talking about?' the teeth asked. 'What is this, some sort of code?'

'—with structural load supports on the overhead beams. And rather than use the original design and leaving the troughs where they are, I've calculated it would be advisable to move them closer to the washing machine. This would give her more space for the new bathroom, and it would be cheaper to erect. Of course, it may cost a little extra for the plumbing—'

'Get that kid out of here! They're talking

some kind of weird code!'

'No, you can't do this!' Ernest shouted. 'I'll tell you what you want to know, but leave Glen! You can't take him! You can't have him!'

Agent 262 opened the door to where the others were, pulled Ernest over by the arm, and pushed him in with them.

'*Noooo!*'

Then he re-locked the door behind him and went to stand beside Glen.

'Okay, you, on to the couch!' ordered 208, holding the gun.

'I will not! In any case, it's too high. I wasn't built for such gymnastics!'

'Do you want me to short you out?' he threatened in a teethy whisper.

'You wouldn't dare!'

'Try me.'

'It appears I have no choice. But you'll have to help me. I can't possibly get up there unassisted.'

Both agents helped Glen on to the couch. Once he was up, 262 went outside to the bus and returned carrying a large black brief-case. Inside it were tools. Very special tools. The kind used in robotics and computer technology. Fine, delicate instruments.

15

A change of heart

'**A**re you okay, Ernie?' Rex rushed over and asked him.

Ernest had landed on the floor in the middle of a small windowless room. It had been some sort of a meat storage room before. There were exposed steel beams running across overhead, some still with a hook dangling down here and there. Around three of the walls was a wide wooden shelf at chair height. There was a single fly-specked light globe above, and a grille set into one of the walls, just below the ceiling.

'Here, let me help you up,' Rowena said.

She took one arm, while Rex took the other,

and helped Ernest up on to the shelf.

'Who do they think they are?' Rex spoke to the door.

Elizabeth, Robert and the others were sitting opposite.

'They want Glen,' Ernest said. 'They want to see how he works.'

'Are you comfortable, Ernest?'

Rowena took off her jumper and placed it behind Ernest's head saying, 'Why don't you rest for a while, Ernest?'

Then Rex took off his cardigan and put it around Ernest's shoulders. Once Ernest was comfortable they gathered around him—all except Elizabeth, of course.

'What do you think we should do, Ernest?'

'Any suggestions, Ernie?'

'What have you got in mind?'

'Just give us the word, Ernest.'

Ernest shut his eyes and pretended he was thinking of something, but all he could see was Glen in trouble.

'Well, what do you think Ernest?'

'Any ideas?'

Ernest opened his eyes and happened to look at the hooks dangling overhead. 'We could try chipping our way out with those old meat hooks,' he suggested faintly.

Rex reached up and took down the hooks from the beams. There were four altogether.

'We could work in shifts. What do you think, Ernie?'

'Yes, all right, Rex,' Ernest said tiredly.

Rex, Rowena, Robert and Pauline began quietly chipping away. The hooks were as rusty as they were blunt, and barely made even shallow grooves in the concrete. Their work set free clouds of fine, coarse dust.

'It's not getting in your eyes, is it, Ernest?'

'Here, borrow my glasses,' Pauline offered. She took them off and her eyes shrank to a third of their size. Pauline couldn't see her way to the person beside her without them.

'No thanks, Pauline.'

'I'm scared,' Colin whimpered.

'Don't worry,' Rex reassured him. 'We'll get out. We've got Ernest with us, haven't we.'

In the next room there was a sharp, clicking

noise. Nobody heard it except the ISIO agents standing over Glen. It was the sound of Glen being switched off at his central power bank. They had found his main control lines.

'Although a lot of good that little twerp is to us,' Rex added. He paused. His expression changed and he looked confused, as if uncertain of what he had just said. Then the confusion vanished and he squinted meanly. He went on, 'Ernest couldn't tell which way he was pointed.' He stopped chipping at the wall and turned around to face Ernest. 'Who do you think you're giving orders to, you dumb little jerk!' He threw the hook down on the floor.

'Watch out, meat head, that almost hit my foot!' Rowena growled at him.

'Who cares about your foot, gravel face?'

Rowena wound herself up and punched Rex in the stomach. Rex collapsed on to the floor.

'I do!' she snarled, dropping her hook. She snatched her jumper from behind Ernest. His head thumped back against the concrete wall.

A change of heart

'What do you think you're doing with this?' she asked him. 'Putting your greasy little head all over it, watching us do all the work!'

Ernest knelt and offered his hand to Rex who tossed it aside and pulled himself up alone. He'd grown pale and vicious. 'Keep your hands off me, Pickle!'

Ernest sat back down in a little huddled ball. He didn't know what had gone wrong, but whatever it was, it had something to do with the two men working on Glen in the next room.

'Well, what are you going to do?' Rowena came over and said. She was standing over Ernest. Her eyes were half-closed so that she was just looking through narrow little slits.

'I don't know,' Ernest muttered.

Rowena kicked one of his shins. 'Don't be so gutless!' she sneered. '*Do* something!'

'No wonder nobody likes you,' Robert said. 'All you ever talk about is your inventions. You're not normal. You're always trying to prove how terrific you are by showing off your inventions, but you never really *do* anything.

You're so boring, trying to impress us all the time.'

'This whole thing is your fault, Pickle,' Colin said.

'Come on, what are you going to do about it?'

'You're wasting your breath, he couldn't do anything about anything,' Rowena said. 'He's useless.'

'He's good at getting on people's nerves.'

'Why don't you leave him alone!' Elizabeth suddenly said. Until then she had kept quiet, but the others turned and looked at her now. 'Do you think you're all so perfect?' she went on. 'Who are you to talk that way about anybody else! Ernest can get us out. You're just not giving him a chance.'

'Pickle can't do anything,' Rex said. 'He's a stuffed animal. He's dead inside. Cottonwool head.'

The others laughed half-laughs. Elizabeth stepped through them and took Ernest's hand. 'Okay, Ernest,' she said. 'I'll give you a bunk up to that grille. It looks like some sort of ventilation shaft. I think you'll fit.'

Ernest looked up towards the ceiling. 'Up there?' he said.

'Sure,' she said. 'All you have to do is get the grille off. There's probably a shaft you can crawl through to the outside.'

'Crawl through?' Ernest echoed blankly.

'Listen to him, he's like a cassette recorder,' Rex said. 'You'll never get him up there. Ernest would never do that. Even if he did, he'd probably die of fright.'

'Then why don't *you* get up there?' Elizabeth asked him.

'Why should I? I'm not going to suffocate to death crawling around between walls. Besides, I don't think it'll go anywhere anyway. It's a stupid idea.'

'You're scared!'

'I'm not scared of anything. I'm just not stupid.'

'Go on, Ernest,' Rowena said in her sing-song voice. 'Why don't you try it? It might lead to somewhere.'

'No big loss if it doesn't anyway,' Colin

said.

Ernest let go of Elizabeth's hand and wiped his face. There were tears making their way down it.

'I can't stand people who cry,' Rowena snarled. 'I hate it, especially when boys do it. It's so weak.'

'But Ernest *is* weak,' Rex said.

'Elizabeth,' Ernest asked, choked, 'could you give me a boost up?'

'Sure.'

Elizabeth helped him up until he could get a grip on the grille face. It was made of woven wire mesh. The gaps were wide enough to fit his fingers through. He jerked it once, towards him. It came free with surprising ease. Then a funny thing happened. When he was looking for somewhere to drop the grille, Pauline came over and took it from him. She didn't say anything, she just took it and leaned it up against the wall. Ernest turned back to the empty shaft entrance. A small cloud of dust had followed the grille out and was floating into the room.

A change of heart

'He'll never make it,' he heard Rex say. Ernest ignored him and pulled himself up into the dark rectangle—then disappeared into blackness.

16

Glad to be alone

The shaft sloped downwards. The darkness filled in around him as he eased himself further in with his elbows. He could feel the walls on either side and the ceiling above whenever he raised his head. The shaft, underneath layers of grease and grime, was made of sheetmetal.

At the bottom of the shaft's slope it turned a sharp angle, did a back U-bend to the left, and climbed again at forty-five degrees, which gave him just enough space to bend around and up into it. He slipped, thudded his elbow against a wall, and a sheet of dust came rolling down. The thick heavy dust went down his throat and into his eyes. It stuck to his face where his tears had been.

Ernest wasn't crying any more though. He didn't feel like crying now. He had to concentrate on where he was going. He had lost all sight of light, and was moving along only by what he could feel.

He reached another flat stretch. It was slippery here, and difficult to manage, and the air was dirty. It tasted used. He made a point of breathing in as little as he could of it. He realised, too, that he would be unable to turn around if he came to a dead end.

The shaft suddenly widened in front of him. He put his arms out and felt around. It ran in two directions: one to the right, the other continuing around to the left. He kept on going left. The shaft narrowed and began running down again. He eased himself over a crease.

Suddenly he was sliding. It had been steeper than he had imagined. He tried braking himself with his legs pushed out against the sides, but it didn't stop him. He was racing, sliding down fast, and picking up speed as he went. He bunched his elbows up over his head as he hit a bump. His hand hit something blocking the shaft. Even that didn't stop him, and he felt his weight push it out of the way. Whatever it was wrenched itself free and he flew through the air after it.

17

⊸ Bits and pieces ⊸

The wire grille hit the floor a moment before he did. The floor was a little less than two metres down, and the grille bounced loudly and then spun around like a large coin for a moment before stopping. Ernest landed beside it on his front.

He lay where he was for a moment. He'd made it! He'd got out, and in one piece!

Suddenly some hands grabbed his arms and he was being pulled on to his feet. He had landed back into the first room, where the ISIO agents had Glen. They grabbed Ernest by either arm.

'Going for a walk?' the one with the new

teeth asked.

His partner peered up into the exposed shaft. 'Don't see any more coming,' he said. 'Any behind you?'

Ernest hadn't heard him. He'd spotted Glen, over on the couch. He was in pieces! One arm was off, and his legs had been dismantled and were leaning up against a chair. His chest was opened up, his head was off and broken apart. He was in a thousand bits, strewn across the floor!

'Glen!' Ernest cried out. 'What have you done to him?'

He broke free of their hold and ran across to the bench. He stood there, looking down at what was left of Glen. The top half of his chest was still intact, but the rest had been tampered with and pulled apart so extensively he was barely recognisable now. Glen was just bits and pieces.

'You've butchered him!' Ernest managed to say. He picked up one or two things and began trying to fit them back in. It was useless, they were all over the room. 'You've killed him!'

he whispered.

'Take it easy, kid, he was just a machine.'

'He was more than a machine. He was a friend.'

'You're a smart kid, you can make another one. I want to tell you though, you'd done quite a job with him. I don't remember ever seeing anything more sophisticated.'

'He was one of a kind.' Ernest's voice cracked and choked.

'We found your transmission frequency, anyway. Smart idea linking it through the electrode output like that. The only thing I don't understand is, why? Why did you have him set up on that frequency?'

Ernest wasn't listening to a word they were saying. All he could hear was the pounding in his head, the one that was saying *Glen was dead*.

'I should never have used you like that, Glen.' Ernest reached out and touched Glen's damaged shoulder plate. It was nothing more than an old piece of scrap metal now. 'I was so stupid. I don't even like those people,' he went on sobbing, as if Glen could still hear him.

'Elizabeth was right. They were never my friends, they never could be friends. It only made me feel worse, having them around all the time.'

'What's he talking about?'

'I need a box,' Ernest said without looking up. 'Something I can put the pieces in. I'll gather him up and take him—'

'Sorry, kid, but you can't do that.'

The two agents came closer, until they were standing side by side at the opposite end of the couch.

'I'm afraid we have to hang on to the bits.'

'You can't! They're mine!'

'We take them with us!' the agent in the singed suit ordered.

Ernest met his stare. He had calculating, threatening eyes. Strangely, they didn't scare Ernest. He simply stared back. After a moment he looked down at what was left of Glen, for one last time. He knew what he had to do. 'Then if I can't have them,' he said, 'neither can you.'

Ernest snatched up the main power-supply line, and pulled it. It tore free of its socket. Then, without pausing, he poked the line's exposed ends into the logic circuits, and they connected. The kick threw him back across the room against the wall. A shower of sparks flew up and crackled wildly out of control. Smoke poured out and climbed in a yellow cloud towards the ceiling. Glen was blowing apart.

'Are you crazy?' the agent with the teeth shouted. He dashed across to unhook the line. His hand brushed an exposed end as he pushed it free, and the shock sent him across to the opposite wall. Then 208 tore his coat off. Glen was now in flames, and he was trying to smother the fire. He managed to bring it under control, but the smoke was heavy and the smell of burning rubber and plastic was almost unbearable. He looked around for Ernest, but he'd gone. In the confusion he'd run back out the way he had come and out in to the street. Agent 208, still conscious, had a decision to make. Either he went after Ernest, or helped his fellow agent. He decided to do the latter.

18

— What agents? —

Ernest found a telephone box six blocks away. He ran there non-stop and had some trouble telling the police where he thought he was. He finally worked it out, and the telephone box had a location number on it.

Then he walked back to the warehouse, crept back down the corridor and back into the room. Glen was still there (what was left of him). The two ISIO agents had disappeared.

Ernest didn't let the others out straight away. There was nobody in there he wanted to see, apart from Elizabeth. He decided that if Elizabeth hadn't been in there he could happily have left them locked in all night. He wandered about, gathering up bits of Glen. Whoever those men had been, they had done a thorough job of dismantling him. They had known exactly what to do and how to do it. Glen wasn't Glen any more, he was just a pile of computer bits. Ernest put his favourite parts into a cardboard box.

When he opened the door for Rex, Rowena and the others, he simply said, 'They've gone,' and went and sat back down on the bench to stare blankly at the box in front of him.

'What's wrong with him?' Rex asked.

Nobody answered, not even Colin.

Ernest stayed in a silent, distant mood all night, even when the police came and began asking questions. Ernest just stared at the floor or at the box, and mumbled yes or no answers.

'He's gone all creepy,' Rowena said.

There were a lot of questions, and Rowena, Rex and everyone else had to make a statement down at the station. The police got so little from Ernest the police chief had to be called from home to come down and help. The chief was a big fat man who was particularly

What agents?

good at getting answers from people. He sat with Ernest in a small, cluttered room at the station, and offered him jelly beans from a paper bag he had every so often. But Ernest wasn't interested.

Ernest told the chief what he remembered about the men in the brown suits, and the chief took notes, and shifted from side to side on his chair a lot, as if he were trying to soften it up. Then he had somebody take notes from his notes, and then an official statement was made. The whole thing seemed to take forever.

It was way past Ernest's bed time when Number Two and his mum finally drove him home. The others had gone home hours before Ernest, probably because he had the most to tell. Number Two looked pale and tired, and smelt strongly of peppermint toothpaste.

'I'm sorry about Glen,' he said in the car.

Ernest sat not talking in the back seat, staring at the box of bits on his lap. Every so often he would pick something out, look at it, then put it back again and stare out of the window for a minute or two. He finally spoke as they were pulling up in the driveway. 'He said to say you should link the battery condenser through the plastic core of your toothbrush, so you can alter the size of the speaker.'

Number Two nodded. 'I'll always respect him.'

'I'm going to miss him,' Ernest's mum said.

'He said to shift the troughs up towards the washing machine so you can cut down on costs and have more space in the new bathroom extension.'

She thought about if for a moment, then said, 'He's right. He's perfectly right. He could have been a great architect.'

'I think I'll stay up for a while,' Ernest said, 'if you don't mind. I'd like to look at Glen for a bit.'

Number Two put his arm around Ernest's shoulder. 'We understand, Ernest.'

19
═◦ Headlines ◦═

Ernest stayed at home for a couple of days. He didn't feel like talking to anybody, and there were a lot of people who wanted to talk to him. News reporters mostly. Number Two had to take the phone off the hook.

Once the story of how two mysterious high technology thieves had kidnapped a bus-load of school children had been in the newspapers, the school was full of cameras and men and women wandering about with cassette recorders and pads and pencils. But the real story was the robot. Everybody wanted to know about the robot. 'Was he really as clever as all that? Could he really move of his own accord? Was he a humanoid?'

The search for the two mysterious men in the dark brown suits was called off even before it really started. They had been professionals, so well-trained as ISIO agents they would never be found. They had left no clues nor any traces of their activities. Their mission had been to destroy Glen, and now that the agents had completed the task, their whereabouts and the reasons for their actions were hushed up. The public would never know.

On his first day back at school, the headmaster asked Ernest if he would mind holding a press conference.

'We've got to get rid of all these news people somehow,' he said. 'They're disrupting the entire school.'

He let Ernest use his office. It smelt even worse with all the journalists and photographers and everybody in there at once. And the windows didn't open because it had been so long since the headmaster had used them that they'd become stuck.

Headlines

Ernest arrived carrying a cardboard box. He sat down and put it on the table. It had GLEN written across one side of it in a red felt pen.

'Is that the robot in there?' a reporter asked.

'Glen's gone. These are just bits,' Ernest said sorrowfully.

'Is it true,' a serious girl with a notepad asked, 'that he could really walk and talk like a human being? Like one of us?'

Ernest thought carefully before he answered. 'Sometimes, if I helped him along.'

'He could talk quite fluently though, couldn't he?'

'He could say a few words,' Ernest said.

'He could think for himself, couldn't he?' a hot-looking man with a hot-looking moustache asked.

'No, he operated on tapes. It just looked like he could think for himself.'

'What did you use to power him?'

'Torch batteries.'

'Not solar?'

'What's that?'

The gathering began to show signs of

restlessness.

'I believe you had developed quite a close relationship with this robot, that you became friends?'

'With a machine?' Ernest asked, surprised at the question.

'Well, could he do anything out of the ordinary?'

'What sort of things do you mean?'

There was a sound of rustling paper and cameras being slipped back into cases, and chairs being pushed back.

'Do you think you'll re-build your robot?' one of the reporters asked, but by this time everybody had gone. The reporter who had asked the question didn't even bother writing down Ernest's answer.

'I don't even remember how I built him in the first place,' Ernest said.

The headlines the following morning read:

Boy Wonder—Robot a hoax!

Robot? Just a Meccano Man!

Robot boy forgets!

Once the press people had gone, Ernest

took the cardboard box of bits and pieces out to the school incinerator and threw them in.

'I don't remember saying you could use that incinerator,' Rex said from behind him.

'You're forgetting yourself, Pickle,' Colin added.

'This incinerator is in our end of the yard. You need permission from us first.'

Ernest turned around and handed the box to Rex, who took it without thinking. 'I'll let you put it in for me then,' he said. 'Thanks.' Ernest picked up his bag and walked away.

'Hold it, Pickle!' Rex shouted, once he'd recovered from the shock. 'Where do you think you're going? Come back here, Pickle, I want to see you!'

Ernest just kept on walking, and Rex and Colin just went on standing where they were. Rex had to shout louder and louder to make himself heard.

'I'll get you tomorrow, just you wait!'

Ernest didn't care. Rex wasn't so tough, not when it came right down to it. He just had a big body and long arms.

20

⊶ The party ⊶

It was Ernest's birthday when he arrived home. Actually, it had been his birthday all day, but he'd been too busy to think about it. There was a letter waiting for him. It said:

Can't come to your horible party. It's bad enough having to see you at school every day, without having ~~to~~ to see any more of you.

Besides ▓ I don't want to fall asleep so ~~early~~ early.

ROWENA

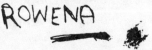

The party

Ernest wrote back to her, stuck it in an envelope, and posted it to her address. It said:

I'm glad.

Then he went inside to the kitchen.

Happy birthday to you,
Happy birthday to you.
Happy birthday dear Ernest,
Happy birthday to you!

'Thanks, Glen,' Ernest said.

Glen wiped his hands on his apron, then limped across to Ernest and handed him a red parcel. 'To my favourite human being.'

Ernest hadn't had a chance to iron out all of Glen's new body yet. And after Glen's dismantling, there had been a lot of pieces missing or damaged. Ernest had managed to replace most of them, but there were some bits Glen was going to have to wait for (they were on order). But most of his new body was there. It was much the same as the old one, but the face plate was a little narrower, and the neck a little more flexible.

The cardboard box of pieces Ernest had

shown to the press and had taken down to the incinerator had been just the damaged bits that couldn't be used again. The most important things, Glen's memory and programming banks, and the central processor, had survived undamaged. Ernest had realised this the first night he got home, after talking to the police chief. There had been enough of Glen left undamaged to put back together again after all, and Ernest had been re-assembling him in his spare time.

Ernest had managed to patch him up into the same old Glen, with one exception. This Glen did not have any facilities for automatic frequency transmission. Ernest had left that out on purpose. And this Glen was going to stay at home, out of sight.

Ernest unwrapped his present. It was a tin of Sparkle polishing liquid, and a piece of soft cloth.

'It's for polishing metal,' Glen said. 'I thought it was something we could both get some enjoyment out of.'

'Thanks, Glen, it's one of the most—'

The party

'You don't have to say anything. I got it for you because I like you.'

All the furniture had been taken out of the lounge room for the trestle tables which were covered with biscuits and little pies and drinks, and other party food.

'There!' Number Two announced to Ernest. 'Catering for two hundred!'

'I don't think we're going to be needing it all,' Ernest said.

'Still suffering from party nerves?' his mum said.

'Well there's always a few people who don't turn up,' Number Two said.

'I'd rather pretend it's not happening.'

'Don't be silly, Ernest. Everything is ready. Relax, you'll see. Come five o'clock everybody will be here, and you'll have forgotten all about your party nerves.'

'It'll be fine, Ernest.'

Ernest opened up his school bag. Inside it was a wad of R.S.V.Ps. This was partly what had been keeping him busy at school as people had been giving them to him all day.

'Everybody is busy this evening,' he said.

Number Two looked mournfully from Ernest's bag to the trestles.

'I think I'll just go and brush my teeth,' he said as he stood up.

Ernest was right. Five o'clock rolled around and nobody came. Before long it was five-thirty, and still nobody had arrived.

'Never mind, I've got something for you,' Ernest's mum said, and handed him a wrapped parcel. It was a book on architectural acoustics.

'Oh, that looks interesting,' Glen said from over his shoulder. 'I haven't seen that one.'

'Yes, it caught my eye,' Ernest's mum said.

Number Two finished brushing his teeth for the fifty-sixth time that evening and came out long enough to give Ernest a steering-wheel cover and an assortment of dental floss.

Ernest and his mum and Number Two and Glen sat together in the living room, among all the food. They were surrounded by one hundred and eighty-five party pies, one hundred and ten sausage rolls, two hundred assorted sandwiches, eighteen bowls of potato chips, eight buckets full of fruit punch, twenty-six plates of cheese crackers, fifty-three bowls of mixed nuts, several hundred pretzels, eighteen dips and fourteen quiches.

'Hungry?' Number Two asked.

'I might go to bed, if you don't mind,' Ernest said.

There was a knock at the door.

'I'll get it!' Number Two leapt up.

It was Elizabeth! She came in carrying a square, book-sized parcel. 'Sorry I'm so late, Ernest, but I had to wash my hair and then it wouldn't dry, and I had to find wrapping paper, and I lost the sticky-tape. I meant to be here ages ago.

Ernest opened up the present. Maybe this was something he could use. It was a book entitled: *Famous Sporting Achievements of Women*. Inside the front cover Elizabeth had written:

To Ernest,
    Someone I've always admired from
afar, your friend,
                        Elizabeth.

Ernest re-read it. He re-read it again. Then he read it a couple more times.

'You know what,' he said, 'I don't care if nobody else comes, I really don't. All the important people are here.'

Number Two wiped a stray tear from his eye, and said, 'I prefer small parties, anyway.'

'I think the Bombe Alaska should be ready now,' Glen said.

While Glen was out in the kitchen seeing to his Bombe Alaska there was another knock on the door. It was Jim Murphy and Pauline, and Robert!

'I got my weeks mixed up,' Robert said sheepishly. 'It's next week that I'm busy.'

'Here, Ernest, we got this for you,' Jim said, and handed Ernest a cricket bat. (Cricket was Jim Murphy's favourite sport.)

The party

'Wheeew! Look at all that food!' Pauline exclaimed. Her eyes were roaming up and down the tables like television cameras. 'We're going to make ourselves sick!'

Pauline hadn't brought anything for Ernest. She wasn't that sort of person. She didn't believe in giving people presents. Ernest didn't mind. As a matter of fact, he was glad she didn't.

'Ernest!' Glen called in from the kitchen. 'Help, Ernest! My arm has fallen off on to the floor!'

'Be right there!' Ernest called back.

GLEN'S RECIPES
Fruity Curried Eggs

You may need an older person to help you with this.

Ingredients:

45 g margarine or butter

1 small onion

1/2 cooking apple

2 tablespoons plain flour

600 ml water

1 teaspoon curry paste

1 tablespoon mango (or banana) chutney

1 tablespoon moist brown sugar

juice of 1/2 lemon

30 g sultanas

8 hard-boiled eggs

Method:

Melt margarine or butter in a heavy pan, add apple and onion and cook gently for 5 to 6 minutes. Stir in curry paste, add water gradually and bring to the boil. Add remaining ingredients (except eggs), cover with lid, and simmer for 20 to 30 minutes. Peel and halve boiled eggs, and arrange in a warmed serving dish. Pour the cooked sauce over the eggs and serve with boiled rice and chutney.

'Ideal for all occasions'—Glen

Glen's recipes

Bombe Alaska
You will probably need to ask an older person
to help you with this.

Ingredients:
1 block plain vanilla ice cream, frozen as hard as
possible
4 egg whites, beaten very stiff
1 slab plain sponge cake
1 tin crushed pineapple
sprinkling of mint

You need the hottest oven you can get. Turn it to the
highest setting and leave it for 20 minutes before
starting.

Method:
Use a board (a bread-board will do) which has been
soaked in cold water as a base. Place a flat slab of
sponge cake, about 4 cm thick, on the board. Place the
fruit (well-drained) in a layer over the cake, and
sprinkle on the mint. Now put the block of ice cream on
top of the fruit. Beat the 4 egg whites until they are very
stiff, and smooth on, making a thick layer all over the
Bombe, leaving little rifts that will go brown. Bake for
3 minutes exactly in a very hot oven.

'A fun party dish'—Glen